Shady Showdown

Carrie Rachelle Johnson

DEDICATION

I dedicate this novel to my readers
who love twisting mysteries

CONTENTS

ACKNOWLEDGMENTS

First and foremost, I would like to thank God for being my Inspiration, my Guide, and the One and Only Lord of my life. I thank Jesus Christ who died for my sins not because I deserve it, but because of His great love for me.

I would like to thank my family and friends who have constructively advised and encouraged me. I also thank my readers who have entered and experienced the various worlds of my novels.

PROLOGUE

ACTIVE ABUSE

Peter Calvin spat out the chlorine water. He smiled happily enjoying the fun day with his family at the swimming pool. The eight-year-old boy swam toward the pool's side. His mother sat at a white plastic picnic table.

Peter used the steps to get out of the pool. "I'm thirsty, Mom."

His mother smiled weakly. She handed a cup of juice to him.

Peter drank it down in one gulp. He sighed pleased at how it quenched his thirst.

"Peter!"

Peter froze. His body tensed at the harsh voice. He turned obediently. What did his father want from him now?

Peter swallowed hard as the older man pointed at the high diving board. It towered above the pool. His heart began to pound as he walked toward his father. Refusing to obey would only result in pain.

His father said, "Up you go, boy."

Peter stared up at the diving board. He reached a shaky hand toward the ladder. He climbed a few steps then glanced down. His father followed him up the ladder. *He's going to make me jump.*

Peter continued to climb. He tried to ignore his fear of heights, but it consumed him. When he reached the top, he stared down at the water.

Peter turned back as the diving board bounced a little. He bit his lip at the sight of his father glaring at him.

"Well, Peter," his father said.

Peter whimpered, "I don't want to, Dad."

"Who asked what you wanted, boy? Jump!"

Peter glanced back at the water far below him. He shook his head weakly.

Suddenly, a rough hand touched his back. His father shoved him.

As his feet left the safety of the board, Peter shrieked in fear. He squeezed his eyes shut. His body slammed into the cool water. He stared at the surface far above his head.

Using his arms and legs, Peter pulled his body upward. Fresh air slammed into him as he resurfaced.

Strong arms grabbed him. His grandfather held him at the surface to keep him from sinking back into the depths.

Peter wrapped his shaky arms around his grandfather's neck. He tried to stop the sobs bubbling up inside of him.

His grandfather brought him out of the pool to his mother's open arms.

"Is he okay, Quincy?"

Peter released his tears at his mother's voice.

His mother took him into her arms. She kissed his head then whispered into his ear. "It's okay, baby. You're safe. I'm so sorry."

"Are you out of your mind, Jonathan Calvin?"

Peter winced at the anger in his grandfather's voice. He turned his head slightly.

His grandfather stomped toward the end of the pool.

His father climbed back down the ladder.

Peter tilted his head. *Why didn't Dad jump?*

"Take it easy, Pop," his father said.

His grandfather. glared at him. He wagged a finger. "That's no way to treat your son. Why do you have to be so cruel to him? Does it give you some sick pleasure to torture him?"

Peter held his breath. He waited for his grandfather to be punched or shoved.

His father growled, "He will never be worth anything until he faces his fears."

CHAPTER 1

BEAUTIFUL BALANCE

Sighing, Magnolia Ruby swirled her straw in her iced tea impatiently. She had planned to meet with Charlie before her friend started her shift at Alice's Diner. However, her heart pounded in anxiety as the time for Charlie's shift came closer. *Where is she?*

Magnolia shook away her worry. Her friend was safe. She did not want to assume trouble had found Charlie. It had been three months of peace for the group.

Magnolia glared at the table. Her mind paused on Peter Cavanaugh. She hated that the wicked man, Charlie's captor, had escaped from the prison van with his henchmen. *That monster could be anywhere.*

Suddenly, a massive shadow covered the table. Magnolia gasped. She glanced up to see who had approached her table. She instantly relaxed.

"Hi, D'Angelo."

"Ruby."

Magnolia smiled warmly. The recovering man was standing instead of sitting in his wheelchair. She peered at his legs pleased by the cane helping her friend get around. "I see you have traded your wheelchair in for a new model."

"Yes, ma'am. I am mobile now," replied D'Angelo.

Magnolia said, "I'm glad. What are you doing here?"

D'Angelo leaned on his cane with a twinkle of mischief in his eyes. He glanced back and forth like he had a secret to share. "Ms. Alice didn't tell you?"

"No. Tell me what?"

"I'm officially back to work," D'Angelo announced.

Magnolia beamed at the good news. "Oh, D'Angelo. That's wonderful. I'm so happy for you."

D'Angelo pulled a stool over to the table. He sank down on it placing his cane on his lap. His deformed face had never fully healed, but he had regained the use of most of his body.

3

D'Angelo had been attacked during a short stay in prison. He had spent time in the hospital. It had been frightening for days as Magnolia and the others had waited for him to wake up. It was a miracle he even survived.

D'Angelo said, "My physical therapy has been helping a lot. I only go weekly now. I should be off this cane in a few weeks."

Magnolia reached a hand patting his arm. "I'm proud of you, D'Angelo. You have come so far from death's doorstep."

D'Angelo lowered his head with a curt nod. He stared at the counter. "It's been tough. I don't know what I would do without my family."

"Family has to stick together. You taught me that," said Magnolia.

D'Angelo nodded before clearing his throat. "Is Gloria as excited about her senior year as D'Quan? That boy talks nonstop about it being his best year ever."

Magnolia smiled at the question. Her mind shifted to her adopted daughter. "Oh, Gloria is a bundle of excitement about being a senior. They've only been in school about a month and she's already talking about finding the perfect prom dress."

"Teenagers. It must be nice to only have to worry about homework and dances," chuckled D'Angelo.

"I know. I hope they can enjoy this time of their lives before things get more complicated."

"Me too, Ruby. Me too."

Charlotte Pearl swiped her auburn hair out of her face. She opened the diner door wincing at the bell announcing her arrival. She took several breaths to calm her nerves.

Alice approached her with a notepad in her hands.

"I'm sorry for being late, Alice. Time got away from me this morning," explained Charlotte.

The diner owner smiled sweetly, "That's okay, Charlie. I'm glad you're here. The lunch rush hasn't even started yet so as far as I'm concerned, you're right on time."

"Thanks. Give me a minute with Mags and I'll be ready to work," said Charlotte.

Alice headed toward the counter with a wave of dismissal. "Sure, honey."

Charlotte sighed in relief. Her panic died down. She headed for her usual booth. Her eyes widened at who had joined Mags. "Well, what do we have here? That can't be D'Angelo Walker without his wheels."

D'Angelo turned his attention toward her. "Yes, the handsome man you see is none other than he."

Charlotte giggled at his funny way with words. She held up a fist as her friend completed the fist bump. She slid into her side of the booth. "Hi, Mags."

"Hi, Charlie. What happened?" asked Mags.

Charlotte suppressed an eye roll at the question. She knew her friend had been worried because she was late. She appreciated having people concerned about her. However, it seemed to happen more often now. "I overslept."

D'Angelo grunted, "Oh? Knight keeping you out too late? I can have a brotherly talk with him if needed."

Charlotte snorted as he pounded a fist into his other open palm. She knew her friend would never hurt Leo. She did like his overprotective nature. *I've never had a brother before.*

"That won't be necessary. He has been an absolute gentleman since we started dating," said Charlotte.

D'Angelo stood up with a nod. "Good. You let me know if that changes. I'll let you ladies have some girl time. Alice will be barking at me to get cooking if I don't get busy."

Charlotte watched him limp away with his cane. She marveled at how much better he was getting around.

Mags asked, "How is it going with Leo?"

Blushing at the question, Charlotte knew Mags was happy about her two friends dating. She had sought Mags' advice to help her navigate this new relationship. *She even gave me Bible verses to help me.*

Charlotte said, "It's going great. I've never been happier."

"That's wonderful, Charlie. I'm happy for you both. I may be biased, but I think you both are dating very special people."

Charlotte replied, "Thanks, Mags. Last night, Leo took me to Le Pierre. The food was so good and the atmosphere was magical. We ate and talked for hours. Then we went to Club Infinity and danced."

"Oh? I didn't know you two were dancers," Mags said.

Charlotte shrugged, "Well, I'm not too good, but Leo dances like a pro."

Mags joined her in a laugh about the rule-following man being flexible enough in his personality to dance.

Charlotte enjoyed her time with Leo. She could not believe they had been dating for three months already. Their relationship seemed to be on track. *I'm glad he loves me as much as I love him.*

Gloria Fairbanks entered the cafeteria with her pale green lunchbox in her hand. She scanned the lunchroom. Her chocolate eyes fell on D'Quan. He took a big bite out of his sandwich.

Gloria strutted across the cafeteria. She dodged other high schoolers as she tried to reach her boyfriend. She smirked at him as he gobbled down his lunch. "Big Mama forget to give you breakfast this morning, D'Quan?"

"No. I've worked up an appetite on the track field in P.E. I don't know why we are forced to run like animals until we are sweaty and famished," explained D'Quan.

Setting her lunchbox on the table, Gloria sat across from D'Quan. She shook her head. She had heard his rant about the horrors of physical education many times.

Opening her lunchbox, Gloria pulled out the components of her lunch. She had a salad, chopped apple slices, and a bottle of green tea. Starting to eat healthier, she wanted to get in shape so she could have the best senior year ever.

D'Quan said, "Gloria, guess what?"

"What?" Gloria asked.

D'Quan's eyes shone with excitement. He gestured with his hands. "I've been invited to participate in the Missouri Tri-County Science Fair in February."

Gloria smiled warmly. It did not sound exciting to her, but D'Quan loved science. "That's great, D'Quan."

"Do you want to be my partner?"

Gloria ate a bite of her salad stalling her answer. She had no desire to be a part of creating a science project for the Science Fair.

D'Quan said, "It's okay if you don't want to, Gloria. I'm not always thrilled with what you like."

"Like what?"

"Chick flicks, shopping sprees, and swimming," D'Quan recited his list.

Gloria nodded, "I can understand that, D'Quan. I'm really not into science so I'm probably not the best choice for your partner especially if you want to win."

"Okay. I'll find someone."

As the couple's other friends began to join them at the table, Gloria sighed with contentment. *This is going to be the best year ever!*

Detective Leo Knight trudged up the sidewalk toward the crime scene wishing he felt more energetic. He yawned recovering by placing a hand over his mouth.

Frankie asked, "Charlie keeping you up too late?"

Leo rolled his eyes. He glanced over at his partner. She smirked back at him. "For your information, we were out on the town late last night."

"Doing?" Frankie asked with raised eyebrows.

Leo was tempted to keep the information from the nosy woman. However, Frankie Lemmons always pestered until she got what she wanted. He had learned that from experience.

Leo said, "Dinner and dancing."

A loud laugh resounded from his partner.

Leo stopped walking. He placed his hands on his hips offended by her amusement. "What's so funny, Francesca?"

Frankie made a disgusted face at him. "Not so loud, Leopha."

Leo cringed at the use of his full first name. He narrowed his eyes at her.

Laughing, Frankie held her hands up into the air. "I'm sorry, Leo. I just can't picture you dancing."

"I'll have you know my mother made me learn how to dance a variety of styles when I was a kid. She said a true gentleman can take his lady dancing in diverse environments," Leo explained.

Frankie said, "I'm sure Charlie appreciates it. By the way, has she met the folks yet?"

Leo cringed at the question. He hadn't even thought about putting Charlie through the torture of meeting his parents. His father would be kind and accepting. On the other hand, his mother was known for being blunt and opinionated. She had never liked any of his girlfriends.

Shaking his head, Leo said, "No. It's too soon for that."

"Okay. Maybe by the holidays. That gives you a couple of months to stress over it, Leopha."

"Funny, Francesca."

Sitting at his mahogany desk surrounded by stacks of books, Peter Cavanaugh poured over a book full of useful ideas. He jotted notes on a notepad. He needed to come up with a new game to defeat Magnolia Ruby and her friends. Peter had been in hiding in the city for the last three months.

Peter fumed at the memory of their previous game. His mind recalled how he had lost. Being arrested had not been part of his plan. However, his secret pawn had helped him escape the van enroute to prison. Peter had been hiding in the city since his escape. *Three long months.*

A loud knock came to the door. Peter tensed at the intrusion. His henchmen had been told many times not to interrupt him when he was reading. Did they have a death wish?

Another knock resounded on the door. Peter set his pen down on the notepad. "Come in."

Peter glanced over at the intruder.

Weldon Hitchcock entered his office.

Peter nodded at his secret pawn. The retired cop had been useful though he would be needed more in the new game.

Clearing his throat, Weldon asked, "Do you have a plan yet, Boss?"

"I'm close. Soon, we'll play a game even Magnolia Ruby will not be able to win."

CHAPTER 2

COMPLEX CONVERSATION

Charlotte Pearl wiped the wet dishcloth on the counter. She hummed happily thinking about her date with Leo the night before. She was pleased with how her relationship with the man was progressing. She imagined their life together from dating to marriage. *We will live happily ever after.*

"Earth to Pearl!"

Charlotte spun around.

D'Angelo leaned on the kitchen window with a plate in his hand.

Charlotte hurried over to the opening. She grabbed the completed order. "Sorry, D'Angelo. I was daydreaming."

"About what?" D'Angelo asked with a smirk.

Charlotte shrugged. Her face flushed warm. How could she answer the private question? She placed the plate down on the end of the counter where a woman waited patiently.

Alice stuck her pencil behind her ear. She moved behind the counter. She hung a ticket on the window for D'Angelo. "I'll bet she's daydreaming about a handsome police detective."

Charlotte blushed at Alice's singsong tone. She turned back to the kitchen window facing her friends. "Maybe."

D'Angelo grunted, "He better treat you like the jewel you are, Pearl, or Knight will have to deal with me."

"I think he can still outrun, you, D'Angelo," teased Charlotte.

D'Angelo said, "Yes, but I can throw my cane at him like a ninja."

Charlotte laughed at her silly friend. Her heart swelled with thankfulness. She had good friends, a great boyfriend, a job she loved, and no horrors for three months. Her life was finally improving from the nightmares of her past. *If only things could stay so happy.*

Sighing in impatience, Iris Lynch tapped her foot. It would have been faster to walk to Alice's Diner. The taxicab traveled down the city street as slow as a turtle.

Iris had been released from Serenity Falls after three months of treatment. Before releasing her, Dr. Sunshine had gave her a warning. If she became violent again, then she would be returned for a much longer stay.

Iris glanced out the window. She hoped to see Alice's Diner in view. She couldn't wait to see Charlie. Maybe her friend would allow her to stay in her apartment for a while like last time. *She has to. We're the Diner Divas.*

Iris narrowed her eyes. A familiar man walked down the street. *Is that?*

Iris said, "Stop here. I'll walk the rest of the way."

The cab driver pulled the taxi to the curb stopping it.

Iris handed him the money she owed along with a tip. She jumped out the door. She scanned the sidewalk for the man she had seen.

Iris spied him. She marched forward to follow him. She could not believe her eyes. *I thought he was dead.*

Nodding, Iris set her mind on the task at hand. *I'll follow him and see where he is going.*

Sitting on her back porch, Magnolia Ruby lightly touched her paintbrush to the canvas adding purple flowers to her meadow painting. She smiled at how the color improved her artwork. The veteran artist hummed to herself. She marveled at how the Lord had guided her hand in another masterpiece. *You always help me make beautiful pictures though not as good as the sunrises and sunsets You paint.*

Magnolia sighed. She thought about the other things God had worked magnificently. She was thankful for the last three months of peace. Her heart wrenched as she recalled the misery her friends had experienced thinking Charlie was dead. She closed her eyes tightly grateful her dear friend had been recovered alive and well. *Now, she's happy with Leo. Another blessing.*

Keeping her eyes closed, Magnolia leaned back in her chair. She thought about her life before Edward died. *I was surrounded by love and family, but now it is murder and serial killers. I wish our lives could settle down for good. However, that's unrealistic since Peter Cavanaugh is out there somewhere. Maybe if he was recaptured and trapped in prison. Then they could have true peace.*

Magnolia pictured her time at the shooting range. The instructor taught her how to fire a gun. She had wanted to learn how to shoot so she could get vengeance against Peter. That was when she believed Charlie to be dead. Her training could still be useful if Peter reentered their lives. *I still have my Glock. I can use it if needed.*

"Nolia!"

Magnolia startled at the loud voice. Her eyes flew open. She jerked her head to the side.

Weldon Hitchcock walked toward her from the side of the house.

Magnolia asked, "Weldon, what are you doing here?"

Weldon wiped a hand over his bushy moustache. He stood at the bottom step of her porch. "I wanted to see you. I knocked but there was no answer so I thought I would check if the talented artist was on her porch doing work."

"Join me. I would welcome the company," said Magnolia.

Weldon climbed the porch steps. He faced a lawn chair toward her. Sitting down, he kept his eyes on the artist's canvas. "That's so lovely, Nolia. I remember going on a picnic in a meadow like that once."

"Oh? Was that with your old girlfriend?" teased Magnolia.

Weldon waggled his bushy eyebrows at her. "Oh, yes. Her name was Wendy. We were both eight years old at the time. Our church had a picnic with food and games. We had so much fun that day."

Magnolia beamed at the pleasant memory. She liked he was sharing it with her.

Reaching toward her, Weldon took her free hand. He kissed it lightly.

Magnolia's face flushed warm at the loving gesture. She set her paintbrush on the easel tray.

Weldon said, "Of course, the next day wasn't as nice. We had a huge storm with lots of lightning and thunder. I was terrified until it finally passed. I've always been afraid of storms."

"They can be frightening," replied Magnolia.

Weldon nodded, "Yeah. What are you afraid of, Nolia?"

Magnolia's mind flicked instantly to her past with fire. She shuddered at the memories that came with her fear. So much had been lost because of fires. She rubbed a hand up her arm feeling the scars through her shirt.

"Nolia?"

Magnolia said, "When I was a little girl, my house caught on fire. My family died and I was burned. Only Wally and I made it out alive. I've feared fire ever since."

Weldon squeezed her hand. "I'm sorry, Nolia. I know it must have been difficult to endure. Let's talk about something more pleasant. I had a dream once that I would swim in a pool full of tapioca pudding. I have always wanted that since I had the dream."

Magnolia laughed at the silly dream.

"And your dream, Nolia?"

"To live peacefully with my family and friends," Magnolia replied.

Weldon leaned forward. He lowered his voice to a whisper. "And your handsome man of course."

Magnolia giggled. She accepted the kiss he gave her. She wrinkled her nose at the bristly moustache. Would she ever get used to it? *I'm glad I've found him.*

Detective Leo Knight watched as the coroner rolled the body bag out of the suburban house. The initial finding of the coroner was the woman had been strangled.

Leo turned toward the deceased woman's husband. He joined his partner.

Towering over the man, Frankie said, "Mr. Holloway, do you have anything to say?"

Anthony Holloway glanced at Leo. He appeared to be highly uncomfortable talking to the detectives.

Frankie leaned forward.

Mr. Holloway leaned back against the couch. His eyes widened at her closeness.

Frankie said, "Confess, Holloway. You killed your wife, right?"

Leo rolled his eyes. He wanted to chastise Frankie for her aggressive style of interrogation. However, he had seen it work. *I'll wait and see what happens for now.*

Mr. Holloway lowered his head. He explained, "I killed her. She was cheating on me. I caught her talking on the phone with her lover. I was angry. I grabbed her, but I didn't mean to kill her."

Leo's eyes widened at the confession. He motioned for two police officers. They hurried forward with handcuffs ready to escort the murderer to the police station.

Leo turned his attention to his partner. "I wish all cases were this easy, Lemmons."

"Where would be the fun in that?"

Peter Cavanaugh growled under his breath. He glowered at his ringing cell phone. He slammed the book he was reading shut. His temper flared at another interruption in his research. Picking up the cell phone, he accepted the call after seeing the caller was Weldon.

Peter snapped, "What?"

"Sorry to disturb you, boss, but I found out what Ruby fears," Weldon said.

Peter's anger faded at the news. He picked up his pen and moved his notepad closer to him. "What is it?"

"Fire. She is terrified of fire," replied Weldon.

Peter jotted down the information on his notepad. "Perfect. Keep up the good work, Weldon. Let me know if she tells you anything else of use."

As he ended the call, Peter reached for the book. He was using it for research to help him with his next game. *Frantic Fears by Lonnie Iota.*

Peter sighed, "Magnolia will never be worth anything until she faces her fears."

CHAPTER 3

DARK DISCOVERY

Gloria Fairbanks giggled at Angelica's story. The two girls exited the school heading home. She scanned the schoolyard hoping to see D'Quan. Maybe he would come over to her house for a bit. She could also hang out at his place. She was sure Big Mama would not mind.

Gloria froze on one of the steps. Her heart pounded at D'Quan standing near the sidewalk talking to another girl. Temper flaring, she narrowed her eyes. *La'Keshia Wallace.*

La'Keshia patted D'Quan's arm. She strutted away swinging her hips dramatically as she walked.

Gloria glared at her boyfriend. D'Quan stared at La'Keshia's departure. Why would he dare look at another woman?

Gloria mumbled, "See you tomorrow, Angelica."

"Bye, Gloria."

Gloria tromped down the stairs. She stormed past D'Quan not even looking at him.

D'Quan called, "Gloria! Hey, Gloria! Wait up!"

Gloria kept walking. Footsteps behind her told that D'Quan was racing to catch up with her. She halted as he jumped in front of her with his hands raised.

D'Quan asked, "Gloria, what's wrong?"

"You know what's wrong, D'Quan Walker," hissed Gloria.

D'Quan shrugged, "I'm not a mind reader."

Gloria crossed her arms. "Who were you just talking to?"

"La'Keshia Wallace. She's my partner for the Missouri Tri-County Science Fair," answered D'Quan.

Gloria's eyes bulged. Her fury increased. She could not believe her boyfriend had chosen the love goddess of the school to be his science partner. Why had he chosen another woman to be his partner? There were plenty of boys in the school who liked science.

D'Quan added, "La'Keshia and I are meeting at my house in an hour."

Gloria's eyes narrowed at the clueless boy. "Why do you have to work on it so soon? The Science Fair is months away."

"It will take some time to come up with a winning idea. Then we must make a plan. We'll need to work together several times before the actual Science Fair," explained D'Quan.

Gloria said, "Well, I hope you two will be happy together."

Leaving D'Quan standing stunned on the sidewalk, Gloria stomped away. She needed to get home so she could cry about his betrayal. *How could he do this to me?*

Charlotte Pearl's heart fluttered in excitement. Her cell phone screen lit up with Leo's name. She accepted the call eager to talk to her boyfriend. "Hi, Leo."

"Hi, Charlie. I was wondering if you were available tomorrow," Leo said.

Charlotte smiled warmly, "Yes. It's my day off."

"Mine too. Want to spend our day off together?"

"Of course. What did you have in mind?" asked Charlotte.

Leo said, "I was thinking about a trip to the zoo."

Charlotte beamed at the idea. She loved animals. The zoo was one of her favorite places. She had not been in a long time. "Sounds fun."

"Great. I'll pick you up at nine tomorrow morning," said Leo.

"Okay. I'll be ready."

"See you then. Love you, Charlie."

"Love you too, Leo."

As the couple ended their call, Charlotte placed her cell phone back in her pocket. She turned back to the kitchen window. Her face flushed. D'Angelo gawked at her. *I forgot I was at the diner.*

Charlotte asked, "Don't you have anything better to do than stare at me?"

"I like to see you happy, Pearl," said D'Angelo.

Smiling warmly, Charlotte returned to her work. She could not remember the last time she had been this happy. *That's because it has been so long since I have been happy.*

Magnolia Ruby stirred the sauce savoring the tomato scent wafting in the air. She reached for a pinch of salt.

Weldon hovered near her shoulder. "You could add some oregano."

Turning her body, Magnolia pushed him back from her cooking area. "I am capable of cooking spaghetti and meatballs without your help. Wally taught me how to cook before I got married. He said he wanted to make sure I didn't poison Edward."

Magnolia smiled at the memory. Why was she thinking about her deceased husband while cooking for her new boyfriend? Guilt formed in her stomach.

Weldon said, "Well, I'm going to cook for you soon. Then you will see I am the cooking master in this relationship."

Magnolia chuckled at his quick wit. She opened her mouth with a retort. However, she grew silent as the front door slammed.

Magnolia hurried toward the living room. Something must be wrong for Gloria to enter the house like that. She halted at the anger on Gloria's face. "Gloria, what's wrong?"

Gloria placed her hands on her hips. "Why are men such pigs?"

Magnolia stuttered at the shocking question. She did not know what to say. How could she explain without knowing what had caused Gloria's anger?

Weldon grunted, "Because we're fools who don't know how to treat treasures like women properly."

Throwing her hands up in the air, Gloria stomped to the stairs. "Exactly!"

Sighing, Magnolia glanced over at Weldon. She raised an eyebrow at his prompt answer to the teenager's question.

Weldon shrugged, "I learned a long time ago to answer that way. Nothing else will keep a woman from turning on you fast and forgetting the man who wronged her."

Magnolia rolled her eyes. "Just make sure dinner doesn't burn. I'm going to go talk to her."

As Weldon returned to the kitchen, Magnolia headed for the stairs. She stopped at the bottom stair as a sudden thought came to mind. "And don't add anything to my recipe."

"Well, shucks. I almost got away with it," chuckled Weldon.

Smiling, Magnolia shook her head. She climbed the stairs thinking about what to say to Gloria. She hoped she could help the teenage girl with her newest crisis. *A mother's work is never done.*

Iris Lynch followed the man down a rundown street. She glanced around. There were not many people in the area. She watched the man approach an old house with broken windows and an overgrown yard.

The man used a key to open the door. He peered around then entered the house.

Iris hurried across the street. She searched for a window to use to spy on the man. Light shone from a window at the side of the house. She peeked into the room finding it lit up with candlelight. Why weren't lightbulbs being used? It was a large dining room with a long wooden table covered with dishes of food.

Iris stared at the man she had followed. He sat down in an empty seat on one side of the table. Other men welcomed him.

Iris flicked her eyes from each man. She did not know any of them until she came to the end of the table. She frowned at a familiar man sitting at the head of the table like the leader. *Peter Cavanaugh.*

Iris' stomach flopped at the sight of him. He had pretended to be her friend at Serenity Falls. She had received a letter from Charlie updating her on the crimes of Peter Cavanaugh. He had kidnapped Charlie and tormented her for a month. Her friend escaped and Peter was arrested though he never made it to the prison. *Somebody helped him escape.*

Iris moved away from the window. She pulled her cell phone from her pocket. She typed on her contacts unsure of who she could call for advice. She doubted the police would believe her.

Iris clicked on Dr. Sunshine's phone number. Maybe the perky doctor could help her figure out what to do with the discovery. She hissed under her breath. The call went to voicemail.

Iris waited for the beep to signal. She would leave her a message. At the beep, she said, "Dr. Sunshine, it's Iris. I found Peter Cavanaugh. He's in an old house on Gladys Lane. He's got a lot of henchmen with him. I'm sure they are up to no good. You won't believe this part. I found him by following…"

A throat clearing loudly behind her. Iris to spun around without finishing her message. Her eyes widened.

Peter Cavanaugh stood a few feet away. He smirked, "Well, if it isn't my dear friend Iris."

Backing up, Iris stopped at laughter behind her. Peter's henchmen were blocking her exit.

Raising his hands in the air, Peter said, "Why didn't you tell me you wanted to play a pawn in my game?"

CHAPTER 4

EFFECTIVE EDUCATION

Wiping the back of her hand across her face, Gloria Fairbanks removed a stray tear. She pictured D'Quan talking to La'Keshia. They looked so happy. Her rage at his betrayal threatened to flare up once more.

A light knock tapped on her bedroom door. Gloria took a deep breath. She needed to regain her composure. "Come in."

Ms. Magnolia entered the bedroom. She closed the door behind her. She sat at the foot of the bed. "What happened, Gloria?"

Gloria mumbled, "It's stupid."

"If it upsets you, then it is not stupid. Did D'Quan do something?" asked Ms. Magnolia.

Gloria said, "Yes. I came out of school and there he was standing at the bottom of the stairs flirting with La'Keshia Wallace. He said they are science partners for the Science Fair."

Rolling her eyes, Gloria crossed her arms. She expected Ms. Magnolia to insult the foolish boy.

Ms. Magnolia nodded, "That may be true."

"There are plenty of boys to be his science partner, but he chose La'Keshia. She's so pretty," explained Gloria.

"You're pretty too, Gloria."

Shaking her head, Gloria said, "Not as pretty as La'Keshia. She looks like a supermodel."

Moving closer to her side, Magnolia wrapped an arm around her. She recited, "1 Peter 3:4. Let your adorning be the hidden person of the heart with the imperishable beauty of a gentle and quiet spirit which in God's sight is very precious."

"You're right. It's what's on the inside that counts." *But D'Quan sees the outside.*

Ms. Magnolia continued, "Lord, we thank You for the many blessings You have given us. I pray You will help Gloria in this time of uncertainty and disappointment. Please help her to focus on the woman you want her to be and not what the world says beauty should be. I pray for her relationship with D'Quan that it would be pure and strong as they keep You at the center. May they treat each other with the love You have for us all. In Jesus' name. Amen."

Gloria hugged Ms. Magnolia pleased by her prayerful support. *I'm glad she understands what it is like to be a woman.*

D'Angelo Walker stretched his exhausted body onto the sofa. He relaxed after his long shift at Alice's Diner. He glanced around the basement thrilled he could walk well enough to go up and down the stairs. The eldest Walker brother shook his head with a chuckle as he watched the video game competition between D'Shontae and Davion. His heart soared with gratitude as he thought about his family.

Suddenly, stomping feet stormed down the basement stairs. D'Quan grumbled under his breath and crossed the basement floor. He sank without a word in his desk chair behind his wall of computers.

"What's wrong, Specs?" D'Angelo asked.

D'Quan grunted, "Gloria."

D'Angelo glanced over at the other two brothers. They had paused their game.

D'Shontae sighed, "What'd you do?"

"Who says I did something?" snapped D'Quan.

D'Angelo chuckled, "Brother, when a woman is angry, it is always the man's fault. What happened?"

"Nothing," mumbled D'Quan.

D'Shontae said, "Maybe we can help."

D'Quan leaned back in his desk chair. "Fine. She saw me talking to my science partner and now she's mad."

D'Angelo exchanged an amused glance with D'Shontae and Davion. They nodded in understanding.

D'Angelo said, "Let me guess. Your partner is a girl."

"Yeah. La'Keshia Wallace," replied D'Quan.

A loud spurt burst from D'Shontae's mouth as the water he had been drinking spewed into Davion's face.

D'Angelo snorted at the yelp of protest from the younger man.

D'Shontae gasped, "Sorry, Treks. La'Keshia Wallace? I've seen her around. She's hot!"

D'Quan rolled his chair around the wall of computers. He glared at him. "I'm not interested in her."

D'Angelo shook his head. He held a hand into the air. "Let me get this straight. Gloria saw you talking to a hot girl who is your science partner, but you didn't tell Gloria. And you don't know why she's mad? Specs, you're a fool."

D'Quan began to stutter through his version of an explanation. However, his mouth closed.

The other three boys blurted out in unison, "She's a hot girl!"

D'Angelo flicked his gaze to the basement stairs as he heard the wood crack.

Big Mama walked downstairs with a large laundry basket in her arms.

D'Angelo motioned to Davion who jumped up to assist the aging woman.

Big Mama said, "Thank you, baby. What's the ruckus down here?"

D'Shontae sighed, "D'Quan is science partners with La'Keshia Wallace and Gloria is mad that he didn't tell her," explained D'Shontae.

D'Angelo added, "And because La'Keshia is a fine-looking young woman."

Big Mama's eyes lit up. She nodded showing she understood the situation. She approached D'Quan and patted him on the shoulder. "Well, you just need to talk to Gloria. Tell her you're sorry and you aren't interested in La'Keshia. She'll understand."

The boys remained silent.

Big Mama climbed the stairs back to the upper part of the house.

Turning the washing machine on, Davion returned to the others with a snort. "Oh, yeah. That will work."

Shaking his head, D'Shontae said, "Not a chance."

"You better find a new partner, Specs, or you're going to have to get a new girlfriend," added D'Angelo.

23

The three brothers nodded in agreement at their advice to the youngest member of the family.

D'Quan placed his hands on his head.

D'Angelo smiled proud of his littlest brother. *His first real women trouble. Specs is growing up.*

Charlotte Pearl brushed her auburn hair smiling at her reflection in the mirror. Her heart soared at the upcoming date with Leo at the zoo. *This is going to be a leisurely day together.*

As the doorbell rang, Charlotte picked up her purse. She strolled to the door. She peeked out the peephole making sure it was her boyfriend instead of a psychopath. *It wouldn't be the first time.*

Beaming, Charlotte opened the door. She leaned into the kiss Leo offered her in greeting. Her cheeks blushed from his affection. *Who would have thought I would ever be this happy?*

"Are you ready?" asked Leo.

"Yes. Let's go."

Charlotte walked down the hallway with Leo. They headed toward the elevator.

Leo talked about the murder case he and Frankie had solved the day before.

Charlotte winced at the fact the husband had choked his wife to death because she was having an affair. She followed Leo on the elevator. *Lord, please let nothing ever ruin our love.*

Suddenly, a classical music ringtone rang out from Leo's pocket.

Charlotte raised an eyebrow as he pulled out his cell phone.

"It's Mom. She loves Mozart," Leo said.

Hunkering in the corner, Leo clicked on his phone and raised it to his ear. "Hi, Mom."

Charlotte crossed her arms. She leaned forward not wanting to eavesdrop. However, her curiosity grew at how he hid the conversation.

"It's not a good time, Mom. Charlie and I are going out."

Leo turned back to her. He held the cell phone to his chest with a sigh. "My parents are in town. They want to have dinner with us tonight. You can say no."

"Why would I say no? I'd love to meet them," said Charlie.

Leo bit his lip. He replied, "Are you sure?"

"Do you want me to say no?"

Leo said, "Sort of."

Charlotte lowered her head with a nod. She glanced back up to tell him maybe they should not date if he is ashamed of her.

Leo planted a quick kiss on her cheek. "It's not you, Charlie. My mother is kind of high-maintenance."

"Aren't we all?"

Leo raised the phone back to his ear. "Sure, Mom. Charlie and I would love to have dinner tonight. We'll come by your hotel at seven o'clock."

As Leo ended the call, Charlotte winced at the lack of enthusiasm on his face. She leaned forward planting a soft kiss on his lips. "Don't worry, Leo. I'm sure we will all get along great."

Leaning his face into her soft auburn hair, Leo mumbled, "I hope so."

Dr. Aurora St. James entered her office at Serenity Falls. She closed the door, flicked on the light switch, and set her purse in the closet ready to start a new day of sessions. with her patients. Many of them had been making a lot of progress.

Aurora turned toward her desk. She held a hand over her chest at the sight of a man sitting in her desk chair. *Peter Cavanaugh.*

"Hello, Dr. Sunshine. It has been a long time," smirked Peter.

Aurora pasted a smile on her face. She hoped he would state his business and leave without any trouble. Her cell phone waited securely in her purse in the closet with no chance of helping her.

Aurora asked, "What are you doing here, Peter?"

Peter leaned forward. He placed his hands onto her desk. "I wanted to know if you checked your messages yet."

Aurora shook her head without a word. She swallowed hard. What could be on the machine that would interest Peter?

Peter pushed his index finger onto the answering machine button.

Aurora held her breath as a frantic voice echoed through the office.

"Dr. Sunshine, it's Iris. I found Peter Cavanaugh. He's in an old house on Gladys Lane. He's got a lot of henchmen with him. I'm sure they are up to no good. You won't believe this part. I found him by following…"

Aurora released the breath as the message cut off abruptly. She stared at Peter who smirked back at her.

Aurora backed toward the door while the psychopath remained seated. She turned startled to find it open. A muscular man with a brown beard towered over her.

Peter snorted, "It's a shame you have heard the message, Dr. Sunshine."

Aurora spun back around to Peter. He had forced her to listen to Iris' message. Her heart sank as she realized what was coming next. *I have to die because now I know too much.*

Peter said, "I'm afraid Iris has made you a part of my little game."

CHAPTER 5

FALLEN FEELINGS

Magnolia Ruby pushed the shopping cart through the produce section of the grocery store. She raised an eyebrow.

Weldon continued to add vegetables to the cart.

Magnolia shook her head at the complicated meal he was planning to cook for her. "I think we need to go to the pharmacy area before we leave."

"Why?" asked Weldon.

Magnolia said, "We may need antacids before this night is over."

Weldon held a hand on his chest with an offended expression on his face. "I'm hurt, Nolia."

Magnolia smiled warmly, "Just in case. Neither of us are getting any younger. Our digestion isn't as good as when we were kids."

"That's true," chuckled Weldon.

The couple continued walking through the grocery store.

As they turned a corner to look at beverages, Magnolia froze stopping the cart. She stared at a younger woman with caramel skin and tight clothes. She recognized her as Felicia Todd. *Davion's mother.*

Felicia reached for a large bottle of whiskey placing it in her cart.

Tensing, Magnolia recalled how the mother had kicked her son out of her home after he was found not guilty. He had been accused of murdering her husband.

Magnolia shook her head. She turned her cart to move away from Davion's mother.

"What's wrong, Nolia?"

Magnolia whispered, "That woman is Davion's mother. She kicked him out. Thankfully, Big Mama took him in."

"Davion's stepfather was murdered by his coworker, right?" asked Weldon.

"Right."

Weldon whispered, "Maybe she had something to do with her husband's murder."

Magnolia snapped her attention back to Felicia. Could she have had something to do with the murder? Maybe she had been an accomplice. Felicia did testify against her own son.

Magnolia held her breath. She had been spotted.

Felicia pushed her shopping cart toward her. "Excuse me. You were on the jury, weren't you?"

"Yes."

Felicia swiped black hair out of her eyes with a weak smile. "Thank you for helping to free my boy."

"If you were concerned about Davion, why did you abandon him?" asked Magnolia.

Felicia's eyes narrowed at the question. She scowled at Magnolia. Would she strike out at her? "Because I was tired of taking care of him. You got kids?"

"A daughter who is a senior this year."

Felicia snorted, "Well, you wait a year or so and you'll be wanting her to leave too."

Magnolia glared at Felicia. Her temper rose at the insinuation. She placed her hands on her hips. "I will never want her to leave for good. You should be ashamed of yourself. You don't even care where Davion is, do you?"

Felicia snarled, "This ain't your business, lady. I'm better off without that punk."

A strong hand grasped Magnolia's arm. She glanced over at Weldon. He pulled gently to persuade her to leave with him before the quarrel became physical.

Magnolia nodded stepping in the direction he was heading. Then she snapped her head back.

Felicia glared at the floor.

Magnolia said, "I can assure you, Ms. Todd, Davion is much better off without you."

The couple headed farther away from Davion's mother. Soon, she was out of sight.

Magnolia fumed at the callous woman's indifference about her own child. She shook her head with a scowl. "She doesn't deserve to be a mother."

Strolling through the monkey house, Charlotte Pearl held Leo's hand. She enjoyed the monkeys climbing through the branches in their enclosure. The day would be perfect except she could tell Leo was distracted. Maybe he regretted inviting her to dinner with his parents. His good mood had changed after the phone call with his mother. *Maybe he doesn't think our releationship will last long enough to bring his family into it.*

"Are you okay, Charlie?" asked Leo.

Charlotte smiled weakly, "I was wondering the same about you."

"What do you mean?"

Charlotte shrugged, "You seem distracted."

Leo turned toward the glass enclosure. He stared at the monkeys without saying a word.

Charlotte sighed, "I don't have to meet your parents if you aren't ready, Leo. I understand."

Leo spun back to her with his forehead wrinkled in confusion.

Charlotte asked, "Have you told them about me?"

"What do you mean?"

Crossing her arms, Charlotte mumbled, "Have you told them about my childhood? Or what Winter Dupree and Peter Cavanaugh did to me? What about my schizophrenia? Do they know about how I struggle with it?"

Leo lowered his head. He remained silent.

Charlotte's heart thumped nervously. Her stomach lurched at the reply her mind envisioned would come from him. *This is it. He is leaving me. We won't be together anymore.*

Sickened by the thoughts, Charlotte blurted, "Are we breaking up?"

Detective Leo Knight's eyes widened at the question. He could see the panic in Charlie's wide eyes. He reached forward taking her shaky hands into his own. He winced at the tears shining in her eyes.

Leo said, "We're not breaking up, Charlie. I love you. Even my parents can't change that."

Charlie blinked freeing tears to roll down her face.

Leo released one of her hands to use his own to wipe the warm tears away. He wrapped his arms around her kissing the side of her head. "I love you, Charlie, and I want to be with you."

Charlie's body tensed. "Then why are you freaking out about me meeting your parents?"

"Because I know how they can be. I don't want you to be hurt," Leo explained.

Charlie pulled back with a small smile. "Then we have to stick together."

Leo smiled warmly, "Deal."

The couple shared a passionate kiss.

Leo's phone rang with a circus theme song. He stepped back from Charlie. He smiled at her amused expression. "That's Frankie. Working with her reminds me of a circus."

Charlie giggled. She turned back to the glass to watch the monkeys chase each other.

Accepting the call, Leo said, "What's up, Lemmons?"

Charlotte Pearl smiled as two monkeys chased each other across the floor of their enclosure. Her heart soared now she was certain

Leo wouldn't leave her. She was thankful for his love, but she hoped his parents would like her, too.

Leo muttered, "Great."

Charlotte turned back to him.

"Lemmons and I have caught a homicide case," explained Leo.

Charlotte asked, "You have to go?"

"Yes. I'm sorry," said Leo.

Charlotte shrugged, "That's the job. I think I'll just hang out here. Maybe you can catch up with me later."

"Definitely. Are you sure you're okay with me going?"

Charlotte said, "Of course. That's what I get for dating a cop."

Leo leaned forward. He kissed her tenderly. He turned to walk away.

Charlotte strolled in the opposite direction heading toward the next animal enclosure. She prayed Leo would be safe and able to return to her quickly. *Please let us be happy together.*

Gloria Fairbanks took a deep breath. She raised her fist to knock on the front door at Big Mama's house. She waited for one of the Walkers to open the door to let her in.

Gloria swallowed hard as D'Quan opened it.

"Gloria, hi.."

Gloria said, "Hey. Can I come in?"

"Uh, sure," D'Quan said moving to the side to let her in.

Gloria entered the house. Her mind reeled with ways to apologize for her rash behavior. She stepped to the side and waited for D'Quan to close the door.

"D'Quan, I…"

A voice cleared behind her. Gloria turned toward the noise. Her eyes bulged.

La'Keshia Wallace stood beside the living room couch. She adjusted her low-cut red T-shirt.

D'Quan said, "She's here to work on our science fair project. That's all."

Gloria glared at him. She flicked her eyes to La'Keshia. "He's all yours, sister."

Gloria spun toward the door. She swung it open and stormed out of the house. She marched toward the blue Honda Civic Ms. Magnolia and Aunt Lucretia had given her for her birthday. She ignored the yells coming from D'Quan. She slid into the driver's seat. *I should never have trusted him.*

Detective Leo Knight trudged down the alley with Frankie by his side. He hated that his date with Charlie had been interrupted by a homicide. He did not understand why the police officer at the crime scene had demanded the duo be the detectives to come. "Okay, Perez. Why are we here on our day off?"

Officer Perez shrugged, "You know the victim. I thought you would want to know what happened to her."

Leo paused. His mind shifted to who the deceased victim could be and how he knew her. "Okay. Let's see."

Officer Perez pointed toward a closed dumpster. "She's on the grouund past the dumpster."

Leo and Frankie tromped over to see the victim. His stomach lurched at the deceased being a woman. He swallowed hard.

The coroner pulled back the cloth covering the body.

Leo's eyes widened. *Iris Lynch.*

Frankie asked, "Isn't that Charlie's friend?"

Nodding, Leo squatted next to the body to search for clues to what had happened to her.

Frankie said, "I didn't know she was back from Serenity Falls."

"Me neither," mumbled Leo.

The coroner added, "Her neck is broken. Officer Perez found this note."

Frankie reached for the plastic bag protecting the note from stray fingerprints. "Let our new game begin."

Leo's eyes bulged. He met his partner's gaze. No doubt they were both thinking of the same culprit. *Peter Cavanaugh.*

CHAPTER 6

GRAVE GAME

Suppressing a laugh, Magnolia Ruby watched Weldon struggle with making the complex dinner he had demanded she let him make.

"You won't be amused by the end result, Nolia," grumbled Weldon.

Magnolia snorted, "That's what I'm afraid of, Weldon."

A loud slam from the front door interrupted the jovial culinary contest. Magnolia exchanged a glance with Weldon. *That can't be good. She went to see D'Quan.*

Magnolia said, "Gloria?"

"I don't want to talk about it," snapped Gloria.

Magnolia winced at the loud stomps of her daughter storming upstairs to her bedroom. "I think I'll let her calm down before we have a talk."

Weldon nodded, "That sounds safer."

Magnolia smirked at him. She swallowed her retort as her cell phone buzzed on the table.

Weldon asked, "Is that your other man?"

Magnolia rolled her eyes. "Trust me, Weldon. One man is more than enough especially when it is you."

Weldon stuck his tongue out. He turned back to the stove to stir his concoction.

Magnolia clicked on a text message from Frankie. She frowned rereading it several times. She had to be misinterpreting it. It could not be true.

Magnolia left the kitchen without a word. She sank into her armchair in the living room. She closed her eyes at the horrible news. *Dear Lord, help us.*

Weldon asked, "Nolia? What's wrong? Gloria wear you out?"

Magnolia rubbed a hand over her face unamused by his joke. He did not know about the shock she had experienced.

"Nolia? What is it?"

Magnolia said, "Peter Cavanaugh killed Charlie's friend Iris. His new game has begun."

Weldon Hitchcock placed gentle hands onto Nolia's shoulders. He kissed her tenderly on the top of her silver head then headed back to the kitchen. Once out of view, he pulled his cell phone out of his pocket. He texted a quick message. *Ruby knows about Iris.*

Weldon shoved the phone back into his pocket. He spooned food onto the plates for dinner.

Nolia entered the kitchen with a sigh. "I feel sorry for Charlie."

Pulling out her chair, Weldon nodded, "Me too. She could really use a break from misery." *Yet, misery is all that's coming.*

Detective Leo Knight drove into the parking lot of the zoo. Fear rose inside him. He hoped Charlie had remained safe in the zoo. Ever since he found Iris and Cavanaugh's message, he had worried about her. *Why did I let her stay here alone? What if that psychopath snatched her while I was gone?*

Leo entered the zoo. He headed in the direction he had left her. He scanned the crowd. Not seeing her in any area, his heart began to pound in panic.

Leo pulled out his cell phone rolling his eyes at not using it sooner to find Charlie. He frowned at each unanswered ring. *Come on, Charlie. Answer your phone.*

Charlie said, "Hey. Are you coming back?"

Leo sighed in relief. By the tone of her voice, she was safe. He thanked God that Peter had not snatched her while he was distracted.

"Leo?"

Leo replied, "Where are you?"

"Penguin house," Charlie said.

Leo turned toward the path to the penguin house. "Wait there for me."

Charlie muttered, "Is something wrong, Leo?"

"I'll explain when I get there," promised Leo.

Leo jogged down the path toward the building. His panic faded as he entered the penguin house.

Charlie stood by a glass tank watching the flightless birds.

Dread covered him. Leo prayed for the strength to tell her about Iris and Cavanaugh's new game.

Giggling, Charlotte Pearl watched the penguins flop off the ice into the cool water. She could tell they were showing off for their audience. She had always loved the penguins the most as a child.

"Charlie."

Charlotte spun around at her name. She smiled as Leo approached her. Her heart began to pound at the frown on his face. "What's wrong?"

Leo stopped in front of her. Taking her hands into his own, he said, "Charlie, Iris is dead."

Charlotte gasped at the news. She struggled to breathe as the world seemed to crash down around her. She stared at the floor sorrowful at the loss of her friend. "How?"

Leo mumbled, "Her neck was broken."

Charlotte closed her eyes. She tried to force her tears to stay hidden. "At Serenity Falls?"

"No. Apparently, she was released from Serenity Falls. We found her in an alley…with a note," explained Leo.

Charlotte's eyes snapped open. She jerked her head up to stare at him. "What note?"

Leo squeezed her hands.

Charlotte held her breath at his pause. *He doesn't want to tell me. Why? Is it that bad?*

"Tell me, Leo."

Leo mumbled, "We're pretty sure it was from Peter Cavanaugh."

Charlotte shivered at the name. Her mind filled with horrible memories of being tormented by Peter. He had kept her trapped in a cell for a month with her schizophrenia medicine. He had taunted her telling how her friends thought she was dead. She swallowed hard at the near escape which could have ended much differently.

"Charlie?"

Charlotte whispered, "What did the note say?"

"Let our new game begin," Leo replied.

Charlotte lowered her face into her hands. Why had Iris been killed in Peter's game? Her tears streamed down her face at the tragic loss. Her heart pounded at the new game of manipulation and torment awaiting her and her friends.

Leo wrapped his arms around her. He whispered words meant to give her hope.

Charlotte's heart despaired past the point of comfort. *The nightmare continues.*

Detective Frankie Lemmons tapped a foot at the evidence room counter. She waited for the police officer on duty to release Iris Lynch's cell phone to her. "Hey, Burnes! You want to get me that phone before I retire from the force?"

An older man came into view with the bagged evidence in hand. He snorted, "You think you will keep your job long enough to retire, Lemmons?"

Frankie raised an eyebrow at him. She had to admit she was impressed by his quick wit. "Nice retort, Burnes. I'm impressed. Now, the phone?"

Officer Burnes handed the bag to the police detective. He returned to his work.

Frankie pulled out the cell phone. She clicked through the screens until she found the call log. "Let's see who you talked to last, Iris."

Frankie frowned at a number with the picture of a sun beside it. She clicked on the phone number calling it.

"This is Dr. Sunshine. You have reached my office at Serenity Falls. Please leave a message and I will be thrilled to get back to you as soon as I can."

Frankie snorted at the sing-song voice with the perky message. She ended the call. Why would Iris call Dr. Sunshine right after being released from the mental hospital?

Frankie checked the time of the phone call. *It was around the time of death. I think I better go visit Dr. Sunshine.*

CHAPTER 7

HEAVY HEARTS

Sitting on her side of the booth, Magnolia Ruby stared at Charlie. She frowned at the despair present on her grieving friend's face. She met gazes with Leo sitting beside his girlfriend holding her hand. *Thank You, Lord, for bringing these two together.*

"Lemmons went to track a lead at Serenity Falls," said Leo.

Magnolia nodded. Maybe Frankie would discover some clue to help the group find Peter Cavanaugh and his minions.

"I can't go through this again."

Magnolia started at the soft whisper from Charlie. She hated the desperation she heard. *This game will be hard on all of us, but the worst for Charlie.*

Leo released Charlie's hand. He placed a more comforting arm around her.

D'Angelo grunted, "We need a plan to deal with these fools."

Magnolia nodded toward him.

D'Angelo glared at the floor. His hands clutched his cane tightly.

Weldon added, "Iris must have found out something. That's why they killed her."

Magnolia glanced at him. She mirrored his weak smile thankful he was in her life during these difficult times. "Any idea what the lead is at Serenity Falls, Leo?"

Leo shook his head. "No, but whatever it is, Frankie will figure it out."

Magnolia took a sip from her sweet tea. She had been around Frankie enough to know she would not give up until the case was solved. *She is one persistent woman.*

Detective Frankie Lemmons frowned at the three police cars with flashing lights parked outside Serenity Falls. She turned her own vehicle off and exited it. She flashed her badge at an officer who pointed out the man in charge. "Detective Lemmons."

"Detective Morris."

Frankie grimaced, "What's going on here?"

"There's been a murder," Detective Morris said.

Frankie gritted her teeth. She dreaded what had happened. "Dr. Sunshine?"

Detective Morris' eyes widened. "How did you know?"

"She may have been connected to a murder I'm investigating. Do you mind if I check out the crime scene?"

"Be my guest. I'll show you what we found."

Frankie followed Detective Morris.into the building to the doctor's office. "How did she die?"

"Broken neck."

Frankie muttered, "Same as my victim. Any clues of use?"

"There was an odd message on her answering machine. I'll play it."

Detective Morris pushed the button.

"Dr. Sunshine, it's Iris. I found Peter Cavanaugh. He's in an old house on Gladys Lane. He's got a lot of henchmen with him. I'm sure they are up to no good. You won't believe this part. I found him by following…"

Frankie sighed as she stared at the floor.

"Does it mean anything to you, Detective?"

"Yeah. That's my victim," Frankie said.

Iris had died because she found Peter and then the doctor was killed because of the phone message.

Frankie jotted notes about the message in her small notebook. Which house on Gladys Lane had Peter been hiding in? *I'm sure he's moved on by now. Plus, that is the longest street in the city.*

Detective Morris said, "The only other clue was a note."

Frankie snapped her gaze upward to the other detective. "What did it say?"

"Here."

Detective Morris handed a bagged note to her.

Frankie read it silently. *Sometimes a pawn must die to get the game rolling.*

Frankie thanked him then headed for the exit. She pulled her cell phone out of her pocket. Climbing into her car, Frankie clicked on the familiar contact.

"Leo, we have a new problem."

Terrence Morris watched out the window of Dr. Sunshine's office. He sneered as the police detective drove away. He dialed his phone awaiting an answer.

"What?"

Terrence grimaced at the harsh tone. "Lemmons found Sunshine, Boss."

"Good."

As the call ended abruptly, Terrence turned to wrap up the investigation. He used to like being a police officer. However, the pay was less than ideal for the lifestyle he liked to live. Working for Cavanaugh had added a hefty amount to his bank account.

Terrence scanned Dr. Sunshine's office for any evidence to point to the killer. *Nothing. Looks like another cold case. That should make Cavanaugh happy.*

Detective Leo Knight ended his call with Frankie. He returned to the booth where the others were gathered. He remained standing to help him break the news. "Frankie found out Iris called Dr. Sunshine before she died. Frankie went to talk to Sunshine, but the doctor was killed too because of the message Iris left."

Leo flicked his eyes to Charlie. Of course, she would take the news the hardest.

Charlie scooted out of the booth with a hand over her mouth.

Leo stepped to the side as she gagged hurrying into the bathroom.

"I'll help her," Mags said as she scooted out of her side of the booth to follow Charlie.

Leo's cell phone began to play its Mozart ringtone. He rolled his eyes and pulled it out of his pocket. He remembered his parents were expecting to have dinner with him and Charlie in a few hours. *That's not going to happen.*

"Hi, Mom."

"Your father and I were wondering where we are eating tonight. You know we like to dress appropriately."

Leo sighed, "I'm sorry, Mom, but we are going to have to reschedule."

Silence came from the other end of the line.

"Mom?"

"We deserve better than this, Leopha."

Leo cringed at the use of his formal name. He took a breath so he wouldn't snap at her. "Two of Charlie's friends died. I can meet with you, but Charlie needs time to mourn."

Leo waited for his mother's response. He assumed she didn't care about Charlie's sorrow.

"We'll reschedule."

Leo rolled his eyes as his mother ended the call without a goodbye. *Some things never change.*

Charlotte Pearl vomited in the toilet. Her world seemed to be crashing down around her again. She squeezed her eyes tightly. She needed to regain control over her stomach. *First, Iris. Now, Dr. Sunshine. Who else is he going to take from me?*

"Charlie?"

Charlotte's eyes snapped open at the sound of Mags' voice. *What if I lose her?*

"I'm here for you, Charlie. You're not alone."

Charlotte moved from her knees to sit on the floor. She leaned against the bathroom wall wiping the tears from her face. "This will never end, Mags."

"We will end Peter Cavanaugh's reign of terror, Charlie. I promise," Mags said.

Charlotte closed her eyes. Her heart burdened with the tragedies and troubles of her life. She sighed weary at the loss. "Why does God hate me, Mags?"

Magnolia Ruby placed a hand on her heart at Charlie's question. She blinked away tears. *How can she believe God hates her?*

"God loves you, Charlie."

Charlie whispered, "It doesn't feel like it."

Magnolia winced at the ache in her knees and back as she struggled to sit on the floor. She leaned against the wall able to see Charlie under the stall door. "I know it doesn't feel like He loves you, Charlie. I know there is great evil in this world which has resulted in bad things happening to us, but I believe it is something else as well." *Please help her understand, Lord.*

Charlie mumbled, "What?"

"I think God lets us go through bad times because He wants to show His love. When my family was killed in the fire years ago, Mama Cora told me God loved me so much He let me live through it so I could be a blessing to others. That's true about you, Charlie. You have lost so much, but it could have been worse. You could have been murdered with your family. I believe God loves you and spared you so you could be a blessing. And you are, Charlie. You are a great blessing to me and the others at that booth."

Magnolia took a deep breath feeling the strength of her words in her own heart. "I believe God wants you to see the truth, Charlie. He wants you to know He is always with you because He loves you. God loves you so much He sent His only Son Jesus to die on the cross for your sins so you can be with Him forever. If you were the only person in the world, Jesus would have chosen to die for you."

Magnolia paused hearing soft sniffles from her friend. She decided to share her own testimony. "When I was fourteen, I asked Jesus into my heart. I prayed to God admitting I was a sinner. I believed in Jesus and asked Him to be my Savior and Lord. You can make that choice too, Charlie."

Magnolia placed a hand under the stall pleased as her friend put her own on top. *She's not offended.*

"Becoming a Christian won't make your life full of easy times, but the struggles are easier to bear when you know God is with you."

Magnolia fell silent as she began to think of a song about love.

"Amazing Grace, how sweet the sound that saved a wretch like me. I once was lost but now am found, was blind, but now I see."

Magnolia leaned her head against the wall. She closed her eyes.

"'T'was Grace that taught my heart to fear. And Grace, my fears relieved. How precious did that Grace appear the hour I first believed."

Magnolia smiled weakly as she thought about the words of the next verse which applied to her friend the most.

"Through many dangers, toils, and snares, I have already come. 'Tis Grace that brought me safe thus far and Grace will lead me home."

Magnolia continued as Charlie's hand tightened on her own.

"The Lord has promised good to me. His word my hope secures. He will my shield and portion be as long as life endures."

Charlotte Pearl sniffled as tears streamed down her face. She had listened to Mags talk about God's love and her own experience. She glanced down. Seeing Mags' hand on the floor beside her, she had set her own hand on top of it.

Now, Charlotte listened to the words of Mags' song recognizing it as the one sang at her family's funeral years ago. She realized the song had meant something different then. She closed her eyes as a strong urge came to her heart she had never known. *Lord, is Mags right? Do you love me?*

Charlotte sighed as a peace she didn't understand came to her heart. *Yes. You love me and I love you. I know I am not perfect. I've messed up many times. Yet, You want me and love me.*

Fresh tears streamed down her face at the truth. *I believe what I have read in the Bible and what Mags has told me about You. I believe in Jesus who is Your Son who died for me. I choose You as my Savior and Lord, Jesus. Please save me and accept me as Yours.*

Charlotte's heart soared in joy as she ended her prayer. "Mags?"

Mags' song ended in the next moment. "Charlie?"

Charlotte stood up. She opened the stall door. She smiled warmly at Mags who moved to stand up as well. She helped her friend to her feet. "Jesus is my Savior and Lord now, Mags."

Mags' face lit up in excitement. She wrapped her arms around her.

Charlotte returned the embrace. Her struggles would continue. She knew that to be true. *But now, I have You to get me through, Lord. Peter Cavanaugh better watch out.*

Peter Cavanaugh read quietly at his desk. He jotted down new notes from the book. He smirked marveling at the ideas he had found for his new game.

Peter glared at the door as a knock came to the wood. "What?"

Remington Holland entered the office. "It's done, boss."

Peter smirked, "Good. On to the next round."

CHAPTER 8

IMMORAL INVITATION

Escorting Charlie home, Detective Leo Knight stood in the elevator next to her. She had announced to the group that she had accepted Jesus as her Savior and Lord. Having become a Christian as a child, he was delighted at her good news. He hoped God would help her feel better in her grief. *Please show me what I can do for her.*

As the couple approached Charlie's apartment door, Leo touched his holstered Glock. Was Peter Cavanaugh hiding inside waiting to attack her?

Charlie unlocked the apartment door. She stepped back to give him room to check things out.

Leo pulled out the weapon. He entered the apartment. Scanning the living room and kitchen, he headed into the bedroom.

"Anything?"

Leo came back out holstering his Glock. "It's safe. Do you want me to stay tonight?"

Charlie smiled warmly, "I'll be fine."

Leo cocked his head. He did not want to leave her alone. However, he knew she would insist. *She's stubborn.*

"Okay, but you call me if you need anything."

Charlie leaned forward with a smile. "I will."

Moving closer, Leo kissed her tenderly. He stepped back opening his mouth to ask about staying to protect her again.

Charlie pushed him toward the door. "Go, Leo. I'll be fine."

"Okay. Okay. I'm going. See you tomorrow."

Charlie nodded, "Definitely."

As Leo returned to the elevator, his phone buzzed. He sighed as he pulled it out of his pocket. *Meet me at 1345 Brinkley Lane.*

"No way, Lemmons."

Leo pocketed the cell phone contented with the plan to go home and get some sleep. However, his curiosity peaked as he thought about the address. Had Frankie found a clue to help them stop Peter Cavanaugh for good?

Leo pulled his cell phone back out texting a reply to Frankie. *On my way.*

Magnolia Ruby savored the sip of hot tea. She hoped to calm her nerves for bed. Her mind reflected on the bittersweet day saddened by the loss of Iris and Dr. Sunshine, but delighted by Charlie's salvation decision.

Magnolia had been praying for her dear friend for years hoping she would choose a loving relationship with God. *You will not fail her, Lord.*

Movement drew Magnolia's attention to the kitchen doorway. She smiled warmly at Gloria and motioned for her to sit at the table.

Magnolia went to the refrigerator pulling out a jug of cranberry grape juice knowing it was Gloria's favorite. She poured the juice into a glass and brought it to the table. Handing it to Gloria, she said, "Now, what happened with D'Quan?"

"I went to apologize for being rude to him at school. La'Keshia was there looking comfy with her low-cut red shirt and tight black jeans. D'Quan said they were working on their science project," Gloria explained.

"I'm sure that is all he was doing, Gloria. I don't think Camella would allow anything too intimate to happen in her house."

Gloria mumbled, "It doesn't matter anymore. I broke up with him."

Magnolia wanted to talk to her more about her decision. However, she could tell Gloria was not in the mood. Her cell phone buzzed on the kitchen table. Was Charlie okay?

Magnolia clicked on the new text message seeing it was from Frankie. *Meet Knight and me at 1345 Brinkley Lane.*

"What's wrong, Ms. Magnolia?" asked Gloria.

"I need to meet Frankie and Leo somewhere."

Gloria frowned, "It's getting late."

"I know. Do you think you could spend the night at Angelica's house?"

"I guess. I can call Ms. Alice."

Magnolia said, "I'll call her. You can pack a bag. Make sure you take your school stuff too."

As Gloria left the kitchen, Magnolia clicked on Alice's number certain she would not mind a house guest. *I wonder what is at 1345 Brinkley Lane.*

Charlotte Pearl curled up in her bed. Her mind whirled with the events of the day. She had enjoyed her time at the zoo until Leo came with the news that Iris had been murdered.

Charlotte wiped at the tears sliding down her face at the loss. Her heart was heavy by her friend's death as well as Dr. Sunshine being found murdered.

Charlotte allowed her tears to fall freely. She recalled how the pleasant doctor had helped her deal with her schizophrenia as well as other issues. She had met with Dr. Sunshine twice since her escape from Peter Cavanaugh's cabin. She had improved after her sessions with the doctor. *Now, she is dead. Both of them are dead because of Peter Cavanaugh. Because of me.*

Charlotte's sniffles transformed into sobs. She closed her eyes releasing her despair. *Lord, please help me.*

Detective Leo Knight tromped toward the apartment building. He swore Frankie had better have an important reason for asking him to join her. A familiar car pulled up to the curb. Leo placed his hands on his hips.

Mags climbed out of her car then approached him.

"What are you doing here?" Leo asked.

"Frankie texted me to meet you both here," Mags explained.

Leo nodded, "Well, let's see what the fuss is about."

As they rode the elevator up to the thirteenth floor, the duo stood silently. Something terrible must have happened for Frankie to contact both of them. How could they handle more bad news today?

Leo and Mags exited the elevator.

Frankie stood down the hallway in front of an open door. "It's about time. You all stop for a late night snack?"

Leo rolled his eyes. "Just tell us why we are here when we should be asleep, Lemmons."

"Fine, Knight. There's been a murder."

Rubbing a hand over his eyes, Leo grunted, "Of course. Who's the victim?"

Frankie gestured toward the open apartment. "Felicia Todd."

Magnolia Ruby's eyes bulged at the identity of the murdered victim. She recalled arguing with Davion's mother at the grocery store a couple of days ago. She listened intently as Frankie explained what had happened to Felicia Todd.

"She was found by police after gunshots were heard by the landlady. We don't know much about her yet," Frankie explained.

Magnolia mumbled, "She's Davion's mother."

Frankie and Leo snapped their attention to her. Then they exchanged a glance full of meaning though Magnolia didn't know what it meant.

"If you didn't know I knew the victim, Frankie, then why did you want me here?" Magnolia asked.

Frankie recovered from her shock. She gestured toward the covered body on the floor. "There's a note next to her body. It's addressed to you."

Magnolia glanced down at a white envelope. She held her breath.

Frankie bent down. She picked it up and handed it to her.

Magnolia stared at the scribbled writing on the front of the envelope. *Magnolia.*

Magnolia swallowed the dread. She opened the envelope pulling out a piece of paper. She decided reading it aloud was the best option since the two police detectives were hovering nearby eager for information.

"Dear Magnolia,

I hope you have missed our games as much as I have. I am ready for a new round. I think you will find it interesting. Don't be sad about Iris and Dr. Sunshine. They got into my business. They should have minded theirs. As for Felicia Todd, it's like you said. She didn't deserve to be a mother. I invite you to join me in my new game. Let's have some fun!

Your humble opponent,

Peter"

Magnolia dropped the note disgusted by his taunt. She turned to Frankie and Leo. They looked equally disturbed by the information.

"We have to find this psychopath before anyone else dies."

CHAPTER 9

JUMBLED JAM

Charlotte Pearl entered Alice's Diner with a yawn. She had slept some during the night though her dreams were haunted by the tragic events of her life. She waved at Alice who returned the gesture then pointed to the corner. She turned in the suggested direction noticing Mags, Leo, and Frankie sitting at their usual booth.

Charlotte marched over with a smile on her face. It faded as she saw the tired expressions on their faces and large cups of coffee sitting on the table. She froze as the three adults glanced up at her. "What's happened?"

Frankie hopped up from her seat in the booth with Leo. She moved over to Mags' side.

Charlotte slid in next to Leo. They exchanged a quick kiss. She focused on Mags. "Come on, guys. What's up?"

Mags sighed, "Felicia Todd has been murdered."

"Who?"

Leo mumbled, "Davion's mother. She was shot in her apartment. Cavanaugh left a note for Mags."

Charlotte's eyes widened at the news. "What did it say?"

Frankie slid a piece of paper across the table toward her. "Here's a copy of it."

Charlotte picked it up reading it to herself. Her heart pounded as she read each twisted word from the sick creep who was enjoying his game. She set it down on the table.

Leo's arm tightened around her shoulders.

"Why would he kill Davion's mother?" Charlotte asked.

Mags shook her head. "I don't know. There has to be a connection, but we haven't found it yet."

Charlotte nodded, "Okay. What's the next step?"

The three adults stared at the table clearly without a plan.

Yawning, Mags placed her hand over her mouth. "Excuse me. I'm going to go home and get some rest before Weldon comes over."

"Frankie and I are going to the precinct. We'll let you know if we find anything," added Leo.

Sighing, Charlotte headed toward the counter to get busy on her shift.

"Charlie."

Charlotte spun around. She smiled at Leo as he came closer with a frown on his face. "I'm fine, Leo."

"I wasn't going to say that," Leo said.

"Okay. What were you going to say?"

Leo mumbled, "My mother called. She wants to have dinner tonight. I told her you needed more time to grieve, but she says they are leaving for home in a few days. She demanded I ask you about it."

Charlotte suppressed an eye roll at his mother demanding anything from her son. She cringed at the idea of having dinner in a public restaurant with Peter Cavanaugh playing his games. She shook her head. "Why don't you invite them to come over to my apartment tonight? I'll cook for us."

Leo placed his hands on her shoulders. "Are you sure? You've been through so much. I don't want to add more pressure on you."

"I'm sure. Tell them you will pick them up at their hotel at seven. I'll have dinner ready when you arrive."

Leo planted a soft kiss on her lips and pulled back slightly staring her in the eyes. "Thanks, Charlie. I'll help with the dishes after dinner."

Charlotte smiled at Leo as he left the diner.

"That was a wimpy kiss. You two in a fight."

Charlotte blushed. She turned toward the kitchen window where D'Angelo was watching her with a smirk. "Shut up, D'Angelo. At least, I have a man."

D'Angelo shrugged, "I don't want a man."

Charlotte rolled her eyes with a shake of her head. "You know what I mean."

Magnolia Ruby rubbed the towel over her wet head thinking about her date with Weldon. She had been tempted to cancel her day with him. However, the distraction would clear her mind so she could come back to the case with new ideas.

Magnolia puzzled over why Peter would kill Felicia Todd. Her eyes widened as she realized no one had told Davion about his mother. Putting her towel down, she reached for her cell phone.

Clicking on the house phone number of the Walker family, Magnolia hoped Camella would answer instead of one of the boys.

"Hello?"

"Camella? It's Magnolia."

Camella said, "Good morning, Magnolia. How are you?"

"It's been a rough night."

"I heard about Iris and Dr. Sunshine. Poor dears."

Magnolia took a deep breath dreading the next part of the conversation. "I'm afraid someone else has been murdered, Camella."

Silence. Magnolia added, "It was Davion's mother, Felicia Todd."

A loud gasp echoed into Magnolia's ear. She heard a kitchen chair scraping on the floor followed by a creak as Camella sat down no doubt to steady herself.

"Someone needs to tell Davion, Camella. I was hoping you would be willing to do that. He's so close to you," said Magnolia.

Camella whispered, "Of course, I will, honey. Don't worry about Davion. You help find the monster who is killing these people."

After thanking her, Magnolia ended the call. Sinking down on the bed, her stomach lurched as she thought about Davion's reaction to his mother's death. *She may have abandoned him, but she was still his mother.*

Detective Leo Knight typed on his computer keyboard seeking any clues to help him solve the cases of Iris Lynch, Dr. Aurora St. James, and Felicia Todd. He glared at the screen annoyed by the lack of evidence. Glancing over at Frankie typing on her own computer,

Leo hoped she was working to find connections between Felicia Todd and the other victims. *Knowing her, she is taking an online game break.*

Leo winced as Mozart began to ring on his cell phone. He narrowed his eyes.

Frankie smirked at him.

Deciding to take the call in private, Leo went to the empty lounge.

"Hi, Mom."

"Leopha, you were supposed to call me back."

"Sorry, Mom. I talked to Charlie and she isn't up to going out tonight."

"But..."

Leo continued, "She says she can cook for us if you want to have dinner at her apartment. I can pick you up at the hotel at seven o'clock."

"Does she know how to cook?"

Leo suppressed a harsh retort. He tried to be patient with his opinionated mother. "Yes. What do you think?"

"Fine, Leopha. We will see you at seven o'clock. Don't be late."

As his mother ended the call, Leo growled. The last thing he needed was to spend the evening with his parents. However, he knew cooking for others might take Charlie's mind off their troubles.

Leo returned to his desk. He hoped his mother would not ruin his relationship with Charlie. *It wouldn't be the first one she messed up.*

Camella Walker opened the front door. She motioned for D'Angelo to hurry into the house.

"What's the hurry, Big Mama?"

Camella lowered her voice. "We need to tell Davion about his mother."

D'Angelo's smile faded at her reply. He nodded and entered the house using his cane to steady his balance.

D'Quan snorted, "It's about time, Rex. We've been waiting for this family meeting to start for a lifetime."

Camella shook her head at him. His sarcasm was based on his strained relationship with Gloria.

"Waiting is good for you, Specs," D'Angelo said.

Camella waited for him to have a seat on the couch. She cleared her throat to get everyone's attention. "Boys, I have some sad news."

Camella braced herself. She hoped to control her own emotions. Taking a deep breath, she said, "We're family, boys, so we need to support each other through this hard time."

Camella focused on Davion. Her heart broke for the newest member of the family. "Davion baby, I'm sorry to have to tell you this, but it is better to just say it. Honey, your mother has been murdered."

Davion's eyes widened.

Camella's heart wrenched. She expected him to deny the news or scream at her about lying.

Davion hung his head silently. He placed it on his arms which rested on his knees.

Camella placed a hand on her heart at his quiet reaction. *So brave. Or used to being hurt.*

D'Angelo mumbled, "We know how hard it is to lose a mother, Treks. It's okay to cry. We understand."

"That's right, brother," added D'Shontae.

D'Quan whispered, "Absolutely."

Silence filled the living room as the family waited for Davion to make the next move. The minutes ticked by without a sound or response from him. Camella opened her mouth to ask him what they could do to help him. However, she did not have a chance as a whisper came from him.

"My mother died over the summer when she abandoned me."

Camella held her breath at the statement. She waited to see what else he would say. She blinked away tears.

Davion suddenly began to sob hiding his face.

Camella moved to the sofa. She sank down beside Davion. She wrapped her arms around him.

Camella released silent tears as Davion returned the embrace burying his face into the grandmother's chest as he continued to sob.

She smiled warmly at her other three grandsons as they moved closer placing strong hands of comfort on their adopted brother.

Camella said, "It's okay, baby. You've still got Big Mama to love you. And the three stooges."

Camella cackled as D'Angelo, D'Shontae, and D'Quan protested her insult. She kissed Davion's head. She promised herself she would give all her boys the love they deserved as long as she lived. *Thank You, Lord, for my babies.*

Peter Cavanaugh stood at the head of the lengthy dining room table. He stared at his henchmen as they sat in their assigned seats. He smirked ready to begin the next round of his game. *The final round.*

Peter said, "Gentlemen, you have your assignments as well as the schedule of events. Make sure you stick exactly with the plan. I don't want any of you messing up my game this time."

The other men in the room nodded in agreement.

Clapping once with a loud pop, Peter said, "Okay, boys. Let's play!"

CHAPTER 10

KINETIC KICKOFF

Magnolia Ruby patted her silver bun. She marched to answer the door. She pulled it open with a smile that changed quickly to a frown.

Weldon stood on her porch dressed in a brown suit with a yellow tie.

"Weldon, why are you dressed up? I thought we were staying in tonight."

Weldon waggled his eyebrows at her. "I had a better idea, Nolia. I decided it would be fun to go to the art museum with a real artist."

"It's seven o'clock. The art museum closes at eight. By the time we get there, we won't have time to enjoy it," Magnolia said.

Leaning closer, Weldon winked at her. He whispered, "I made some arrangements with the management to have a private tour tonight."

Magnolia smiled warmly thrilled by the effort he had put into their date. "Well, let's go." *This is going to be memorable.*

Biting her lip, Charlotte Pearl pulled the roasting pan from the oven. She checked the meat thermometer. The chicken was at 165 degrees Fahrenheit. *Perfect.*

Charlotte pulled the metal meat thermometer from the thigh of the chicken and set it into the sink of warm soapy water with the other utensils and dishes she had used while cooking. She glanced at the clock on her microwave. *6:30*

Her heart beat fiercely. She couldn't believe she would be meeting Leo's parents soon. *I hope they like me.*

Wanting to calm her nerves by staying busy, Charlotte marched toward the kitchen sink to do the dishes before her guests arrived.

She smiled at the idea of Leo only having to do the dinner plates and silverware after they ate their meal.

Charlotte plunged her hands into the water annoyed the soap bubbles were fading quickly. *I should have bought a better dish detergent.*

Charlotte froze at a creak behind her. She spun around then shrieked.

A masked intruder raced toward her. He grabbed her around the neck with both hands. He shoved her backwards against the front of the sink.

Screaming, Charlotte kicked at her attacker.

Keeping a firm grip on the front of her neck with one hand, the attacker used the other hand to lift her body. He jerked her head down until it went under the water.

Charlotte struggled as realization covered her. *He's going to drown me!*

Detective Leo Knight grumbled under his breath as he left the precinct to pick up his parents at their hotel. He had meant to leave earlier, but he had been consumed by his research for the case.

Frankie had left an hour ago talking about getting a pie sandwich at Alice's Diner.

Leo shook his head at his constantly hungry partner. He had watched her eat a bag of chips, cookies, and the last of the doughnuts in the lounge less than an hour ago.

Leo scanned the parking lot seeing no one. He walked toward the end of the lot where he had parked his car. He thought about his evening with Charlie and his parents. Reaching his car, he put the key into the lock. He prayed his mother would be on her best behavior.

Suddenly, a scented cloth was placed over his face covering his nose and mouth. Leo fought against the ambush as a chemical wafted into his lungs. His eyes darted around the parking lot distressed at its emptiness. He struggled to stay wake the longer the cloth remained on his face. *Cavanaugh.*

Detective Frankie Lemmons licked her fingers as she finished her apple pie sandwich. Nothing tasted better than a piece of pie piled on the top of a cheeseburger. Her grandpa had invented it when he was a police detective many years ago. Then he named it a Frankie special after his only granddaughter. *I miss you every day, Pops.*

Frankie pulled out her money adding a tip. "Thanks, Alice. See you later."

Alice beamed, "Have a good night, Detective."

Frankie hummed to herself as she headed toward her car. She wanted to get home in time to watch her favorite television show which came on at seven o'clock. *It's the season premiere. I can't miss it!*

Suddenly, strong hands grabbed her arms. Dropping her keys, Frankie yelped in surprise. She jerked her head back and forth seeing two masked assailants holding onto her.

Frankie kicked at the legs of her attackers who grunted before picking her up. Her eyes darted around seeing a man on his cell phone pointing in her direction. *Probably calling the police. They better hurry.*

Hearing a click, Frankie glanced over to a third masked person putting her key in the trunk lock. Her eyes widened as her car trunk was opened. She screamed struggling against the two attackers as she realized what the henchmen had planned for her. Her body was thrown into the trunk floor before the door slammed down above her.

Frankie slammed her fists on the trunk lid. Panic filled her. She blinked her eyes at the lack of light in the trunk. *I gotta get out of here fast.*

D'Angelo Walker stared at the television set as the comedian continued to tell jokes. His heart was heavy at the loss Davion was facing though the boy seemed to be calming down.

D'Angelo glanced over at his adopted brother staring at the floor instead of the television. *He's dwelling on her. His grief won't be over any time soon.*

Suddenly, a loud bang resounded on the front door. D'Angelo snapped his attention to it. What in the world?

Four men rushed into the house with automatic rifles pointed at the family.

One of the men yelled, "Nobody move!"

D'Angelo glared at the speaker. He recognized Remington Holland from their encounter three months ago. He longed to pound the fool into a limp pile on the floor. However, he knew keeping Big Mama and his brothers safe was his mission. *These fools better watch out.*

Magnolia Ruby stared at a massive tapestry of a mountain with a colorful field of wildflowers at the base of it. Her eyes widened at the size of the piece of art.

"What do you think, Nolia?"

Magnolia whispered, "I feel like I'm standing at the foot of a real mountain. This is amazing."

"It's okay. I like your paintings better," Weldon said.

Magnolia narrowed her eyes at him. He rubbed his moustache and stared at the mountain tapestry.

Magnolia said, "Don't tease, Weldon."

"I'm not. You are a very talent artist. You have an eye for detail."

Magnolia froze at his reply which mirrored what her deceased husband used to say to her. *You have an eye for detail, Mags.*

"Nolia? Did I say something wrong?"

Stunned, Magnolia shook her head recovering from her memory moment. She smiled weakly at him and walked on to the next masterpiece. "No. I'm fine."

Magnolia tilted her head at a jumbled painting that did not seem to have a theme to it.

"There is a new exhibit at the end of the hallway. It's a room with glow in the dark art," Weldon said.

Magnolia nodded, "Sounds interesting. Should we head that way?"

Weldon took her hand and kissed it with his bristly moustache. He led her down the hallway toward a red door at the end.

Magnolia stepped to the side as Weldon opened the door. She winced at the small size of the room which looked more like a closet.

"Ladies first. I'll wait until you are finished."

Nodding, Magnolia entered the room. She read the instructions on the wall which hung above the light switch.

"Ready?"

Magnolia turned to look at Weldon. "Yes."

As he closed the door so it could become completely dark, Magnolia sighed in contentment. *What a perfect evening!*

CHAPTER 11

LIMITED LIBERTY

As the room darkend and lime green shapes appeared on the walls, Magnolia Ruby's eyes widened in delight. She suppressed a squeal at the amazing artwork. She had never seen anything like it before. After enjoying the art for several minutes, she turned on the light switch. She walked to the door and grasped the knob. *Weldon has to see this.*

Magnolia turned the doorknob and pushed on the door. It would not open. She pushed harder. "Weldon? Weldon, the door's stuck. Help me!"

Magnolia leaned against the door. She listened for any sounds. She winced at the silence from the other side.

Magnolia took a deep breath forcing herself to refrain from panicking. *I have my phone. I'll call for help.*

Magnolia clicked on Leo's number. She waited for her friend to answer her call. She bit her lip as the phone went to voicemail. She ended the call then dialed Frankie.

Magnolia's heart began to pound rapidly as Frankie's phone also went to voicemail. She swallowed hard. Would any of her friends answer? *I have a bad feeling about this. What is going on?*

Groaning, Detective Leo Knight opened his eyes. He shook his head not liking the dizziness piercing his vision. He blinked several times then scanned the area around him. It was an empty warehouse. *Where am I?*

Leo moved his body finding he couldn't budge. He glanced down. Thick ropes tied him to a chair.

"Hello, Detective Knight."

Leo flicked his gaze at the voice. His eyes widened at a familiar man approached him. "Guard Simmons?"

Simmons had been a guard in the prison where D'Angelo was attacked. He had been the one to tell him about Luther Craven's death days later.

Leo glared at Simmons. He had trusted him. Was there anyone he could trust besides his friends?

Simmons said, "I'm glad you remember me, Detective."

"What's going on?" Leo demanded.

Simmons explained, "You're part of Peter Cavanaugh's game of fear. Each of you will face your fears tonight."

Leo grimaced at the information. He didn't like the idea the others could be in danger. *I have to get to them.*

Leo said, "What are you going to do with me?"

Simmons tapped around on his cell phone as if ignoring him. "We wait."

"For what?"

Simmons shrugged, "Your fear is losing Charlie. We wait until I receive a text she is dead."

Leo's stomach lurched at the plan. He struggled violently against his bonds eager to escape. *I have to save Charlie!*

With her back aching from being forced against the sink's edge, Charlotte Pearl jerked her body frantically hoping to bring her headup out of the water. Her attacker was too strong. He held her up off the floor with one arm while holding her head under the water with the other.

Charlotte reached backwards with her hands into the water. Maybe she could find the stopper and drain the water. She had no idea what she would do then. Getting air was her first priority. Her fingers touched something metal. She tried to twist it and drain the water then realized it was not the stopper. *A knife?*

Charlotte grasped a round circle flat against her hand. Her mind tried to understand what she had found. She tightened her grip as the air began to leave her. She could not wait any longer.

Charlotte desperately jabbed her hand out of the water. She prayed the metal object would hurt her attacker. If he released her in pain, then she could escape the water. She winced as the end of the object hit something.

Suddenly, the hand on Charlotte's throat released her. The other arm lowered from her back. The lower half of her body succumbed to gravity. Her head raised out of the water.

Charlotte fell to the floor gasping for air. She sobbed thankful for at least a brief moment of freedom. She feared the attack was not over. *Lord, help me!*

Screaming, Detective Frankie Lemmons pounded her fists on the inside of her car trunk. Her heart pounded fiercely as the walls seemed to be closing in on her. *There must be someone out there who can help me.*

Frankie yelled, "Help! Please let me out!"

Hearing no reply, Frankie curled her body into a ball. She closed her eyes. She wrung her hands against her chest as her fear increased. *No one will find me until I'm dead.*

D'Angelo Walker glared at Cavanaugh's henchmen. They finished tying the Walker family to chairs in the basement. He glanced around the circle of chairs. Fear was plastered on each of his family member's faces. *I have to be brave for them.*

Remington Holland moved to the center of the chair circle.

Big Mama asked, "Why are you doing this?"

D'Angelo glanced across the circle.

Big Mama was tied to one of her kitchen chairs. Tears shone in his grandmother's eyes.

Remington said, "Peter Cavanaugh wanted to play a game of fear tonight with all of you. You and all your friends have to face your fears."

D'Angelo cringed at the news. He hated what he dreaded was about to happen. What could their fears be? His fear was simple. *The death of someone in my family.*

Remington smirked, "And what you fear, Walkers, is losing each other."

One of the henchmen handed an old-time revolver to the leader of the group.

D'Angelo held his breath. Was Remington going to kill all of them? Maybe he could volunteer to save the rest of the family.

Remington loaded a bullet into one chamber before spinning the cylinder.

D'Angelo's heart thumped at the truth. *Oh, no!*

Remington sneered, "Let's play a little game of Russian roulette."

CHAPTER 12

MANIC MAYHEM

Panting, Charlotte Pearl begged for fresh air to enter her aching lungs. She rubbed a hand over her wet face swiping her auburn hair out of her eyes. *I have to get out of here. If I can.*

Charlotte glanced around her kitchen. Where was her attacker? She cringed at the masked person lying on the floor a few feet away. Her metal meat thermometer stuck out of his neck. Her eyes bulged at the crimson pool of blood growing on the floor.

Gagging, Charlotte moved to her knees. She reached for her white plastic trashcan. Closing her eyes, she vomited. The truth hit her hard. *I killed him.*

Though she hated to have killed him, Charlotte thanked God for saving her from being the dead one. She spat out the vomit-flavored spit in her mouth.

Charlotte wiped her mouth. She prayed for a steady stomach. She glanced over at the dead attacker. She crawled across the floor. Who was the masked person? No doubt Peter had sent him to kill her. She needed to reveal the identity of who she killed. She reached for the black mask with both hands pulling it up the face.

Charlotte gasped. She recognized the man lying dead on her kitchen floor. *Luther Craven? He's supposed to be dead already.*

Suddenly, a loud beep echoed through the room. Charlotte jumped at the sudden noise. She lowered her eyes to Craven's pocket. It had to be his cell phone.

Charlotte retrieved the device. She touched the screen bringing the cell phone to life. A speech bubble at the top of the screen showed he had a text message. Who was texting him? Did it have something to do with her?

Swallowing hard, Charlotte clicked on the speech bubble. She read the text message.

Is Charlie dead yet?

Charlotte bit her lip. Someone expected a response from Luther. If no reply came, would someone else come to kill her? She could not risk facing another attacker. She had barely survived Luther.

Tapping the keys on the phone, she texted a reply.

Yes. Drowned in her sink.

Detective Leo Knight glared at Simmons as he texted someone on his cell phone. He waited for an explanation of what was going on now. He struggled against the ropes determined to find a way to escape his bonds so he could rescue Charlie.

A ding echoed through the warehouse. Simmons read the reply. He nodded then lowered the cell phone back into his pocket. "She's dead."

Leo's heart wrenched at the news. Lowering his head, he forced his tears to remain hidden while he was in the presence of Cavanaugh's henchman.

Simmons said, "Luther Craven drowned her in her sink."

Leo's eyes widened at the information that Craven was alive. Both men had deceived him as well as the legal system. He raised his head glaring at Simmons.

As his temper flared, Leo jerked his body attempting to escape. He wanted to pound the other man to death with his fists.

Simmons held up a cloth.

Leo froze.

Simmons said, "Lucky for you, Knight, your greatest fear is losing Charlie, so we aren't going to kill you."

Leo struggled once more.

Simmons stepped forward with the cloth in hand. He slapped the fabric onto Leo's face then held it firmly in place with both hands.

As the chemical entered his nose, Leo closed his eyes. His mind blurred as he slipped back into unconsciousness.

Alice Scott approached her diner window at rushed movement in the parking lot. Leaning forward, she gasped.

Two masked men tossed Frankie into the trunk of her car.

Alice hurried toward her office in the back room. Tapping her foot, she dialed 9-1-1 and waited for the dispatcher to answer.

"9-1-1. What is your emergency?"

Alice exclaimed, "This is Alice Scott at Alice's Diner. I just witnessed two masked men put Detective Frankie Lemmons into the trunk of her car. We need police to come immediately. I'm afraid the detective is being kidnapped."

As she ended the call, Alice rushed back to the front door of the diner. She peered out at Frankie's car. The men were no longer visible.

Alice swung the door open and jogged toward the detective's vehicle. Her heart pounded as she glanced from side to side for any sign of trouble. A few people had gathered though none were getting involved in helping the detective. *Heartless people. Why don't they try to help?*

As she reached the car, Alice rapped her knuckle on the metal. She leaned down to listen. "Detective, don't worry. I'm going to get you out and the police are coming."

No response came at her words. Had the masked men killed Frankie while she was in her office calling the police?

Alice glanced at the lock of the trunk. She searched the ground hoping to see the keys.

"I got the keys, lady. They threw them in that dumpster."

Alice turned to a teenage boy. He held the keys out to her. Thanking him, she took them and placed each key into the lock until she found the right one. She pulled on the lid opening it. Her eyes widened at the sight of Frankie curled into the fetal position with her eyes closed. "Frankie! You're free, Detective. Open your eyes. You're safe."

Alice shook Frankie trying to gain her attention.

Frankie opened her eyes. She raised her head slightly to look around. Her eyes focused on Alice. She took several deep breaths.

Smiling, Alice said, "It's okay, Detective. They're gone. You're safe."

Detective Frankie Lemmons sat up slowly taking in her surroundings. She gulped in deep breaths of fresh air not liking the shakiness of her body. She climbed out of the trunk of the car.

Alice kept her hands on her arms to help her.

Frankie stared at her. Her heart continue to pound unable to forget the fear from being trapped inside the trunk. *She saved me.*

Blinking away tears, Frankie threw her arms around her. "Thank you so much, Ms. Alice. Thank you."

Alice returned the embrace. She patted her back. "Of course, honey. You're welcome. I'm sure that was quite frightening."

Releasing her, Frankie said, "It was. I'm afraid of cramped spaces. When I was a kid, I was playing hide-and-seek with my best friend Dylan. I got accidentally locked in a trunk. It took a while for my family to find me. I've been scared of being trapped in small spaces since."

Frankie averted her gaze. A police car sped into the parking lot. She did not want anyone else to know how much the ordeal had affected her. She prided herself on being tough and fearless. This event would ruin her reputation.

Frankie whispered, "Ms. Alice, if you could keep my fear to yourself, I would appreciate it."

"Of course, Detective."

"Thanks. And it's Frankie."

Magnolia Ruby groaned at her dying cell phone. She needed to call the police, but there was not enough power left in the battery. *I meant to charge it before my date. I ran out of time.*

Magnolia sat down on the floor determined to use her problem-solving skills and eye for detail to figure out a plan of escape. She considered the idea that Weldon had anything to do with her trapped situation. *Did he lock me in here? Or did someone knock him out and lock me in?*

Magnolia folded her hands in her lap. Her mind replayed the events over the last couple of days. She remembered Felicia Todd and the note. Her eyes bulged as she recalled what Peter had written. *She didn't deserve to be a mother.*

Magnolia swallowed the bile threatening to rise. She had said the same thing at the grocery store after her quarrel with Davion's mother. Only Weldon knew what she had said. She rubbed a hand over her face. This epiphany meant only one thing. *Weldon is working for Peter Cavanaugh.*

Magnolia had dismissed the theory three months ago when Weldon had convinced her he was on her side. She shook her head not wanting to believe it. However, only she, Weldon, and Gloria knew about their date to the art museum. *True, someone could have followed us, but what if Weldon has been playing me all this time? Did he let Cavanaugh know we were here? Or did he lock me in himself? But why lock me in? What does that accomplish?*

Magnolia's nose wrinkled at a new smell wafting under the crack at the bottom of the door. Her brain tried to place it. It smelled like when her neighbor burned leaves or when Gloria had tried to bake cookies. *She burned them.*

Magnolia rose to her feet. Panic flowed over her. She backed up consumed by a familiar fear she had experienced in the past. *Lord, help me! There's a fire!*

D'Angelo Walker gritted his teeth. He listened to Remington Holland explain the rules of Russian roulette. His temper grew at how jovial the man seemed to be at the idea of torturing the family.

Remington said, "I will pull the trigger at each of you until the hidden bullet kills one of you. Then the rest of you live with the torment of losing your loved one. It's an easy game to play."

Big Mama cleared her throat. "Sir?"

D'Angelo flicked his eyes to her. Anguish covered her weathered face. He hated to see her in such agony.

Remington turned to face her.

Big Mama pleaded, "Please, sir, kill me. That will torment these boys more than if they lose anyone else. Take my life."

As the other three boys protested in a loud burst of noise, D'Angelo stared at his grandmother in awe at the love she had for her children. *Yes. We are her children. She is our mother.*

Shaking his head, Remington said, "Sorry, lady. I have my orders. Peter Cavanaugh wants us to play Russian roulette. I've learned my lesson about defying his orders. Now, we'll start with the youngest. That would be you, Four Eyes."

D'Angelo struggled against his ropes.

Remington faced D'Quan. He raised the revolver pointing it at his forehead.

D'Quan's eyes widened more than normal behind his thick lensed glasses. He held his breath.

Silence. Remington pulled the trigger. A loud click was the only result.

D'Angelo released his breath in a loud huff. He smiled weakly at D'Quan. His brother relaxed slightly.

Remington said, "Lucky boy. Okay. The one with the dead mother. You're next."

Davion sat up straighter. He glared at the revolver aimed at his head.

D'Angelo stared at him. He marveled at the bravery of his adopted brother. He bit his lip.

Remington pulled the trigger for the second time. *Nothing.*

"Well, two lucky boys. Let's see if Junkie is as lucky."

D'Angelo turned his head to D'Shontae on his right side.

With his eyes closed, D'Shontae's silent tears streamed down his face. He had survived so much in his short life. Would he live another day?

D'Angelo longed to hug him with words of comfort. Yet, no words would help. He prayed for another empty chamber.

Remington pressed the barrel of the revolver to D'Shontae's forehead. He placed his finger on the trigger then squeezed it without hesitation.

As a third click resounded in the basement, D'Angelo smirked in delight. He stared evenly as the fool turned toward him with the revolver.

Remington asked, "What do you think, Big D? Are you going to be as lucky as your brothers?"

"I hope not," grunted D'Angelo.

Remington aimed the revolver at his head.

Big Mama shrieked, "No! Please no! Kill me! Don't kill my baby!"

D'Angelo's heart broke at her strangled cries as she begged for his life to be spared. He closed his eyes. He hated for his family to suffer at his loss. However, he made a desperate plea of his own. *Lord, please let the bullet be for me.*

CHAPTER 13

NAGGING NERVES

Groaning, Detective Leo Knight began to regain consciousness. He held a hand to his face to shield his eyes from a bright light. He was no longer restrained.

Leo opened his eyes more fully. He sat in his SUV a few feet behind a bright street light. Narrowing his eyes, he glanced around attempting to identify his location. He was parked outside Charlie's apartment building. *Simmons wanted me to see her dead body.*

Leo climbed out of the car. He held onto the door to regain his balance on shaky legs. He hobbled toward the building not wanting to see Charlie's drowned body, but he longed to hold her one last time.

Leo entered the building and trudged into the elevator forcing his tears to stay contained until he held Charlie in his arms.

Leo recalled the memory of what his life had become the last time he thought Charlie was dead. He pictured the collection of beer bottles littering his coffee table. He had avoided his friends not wanting any comfort.

Leo swore he would not relive that experience. *I will cling to Mags, Frankie, and the Walkers. They're my family too. We will have to help each other grieve. Again.*

As the elevator opened, Leo took a deep breath trying to steady his shattered nerves. He stopped outside Charlie's apartment. He did not have a key.

Leo considered convincing the landlady to give him one. She would probably help a police detective. However, his frustration and anger rose at the thought of his sweet Charlie lying dead on the floor as if she had no one. *You have me, Charlie. Always.*

Leo slammed his foot into the wood of the door. It splintered but remained intact. He froze at the sound of a feminine scream from inside. *It can't be!*

Leo kicked the door once more. It opened fully. He entered the apartment with his heart racing in hope.

"Charlie!"

Leo's eyes filled with relieved tears.

Charlie stood up from behind her table in the kitchen. Her hair and clothes were wet. Blood covered her hands.

Leo raced forward. He placed his hands on her shoulders and examined her for injuries.

Charlie whispered, "It's not my blood."

Leo frowned at the news. He opened his mouth to ask for details. However, he was suddenly engulfed in a tight embrace.

Charlie wrapped her arms around him. She sobbed into his chest.

Leo returned the hug kissing the side of her wet head. "You're safe, Charlie. I'm here."

Charlie sobbed even harder.

Leo held her tighter.

Charlie cried, "I killed him, Leo. He was trying to drown me. I found a meat thermometer in the sink. I hit him with it in the neck and he died."

Pulling back, Leo wiped the tears from her face with his hands. "It's okay, Charlie. Stay here."

Leo pulled out his cell phone. Moving around the kitchen table, he dialed the precinct. There was a massive amount of blood near the dead man's head.

Leo spoke quietly to the dispatcher. He reported the situation. He was informed that a team of police officers and the coroner would be heading for Charlie's apartment. Ending the call, he knelt beside the body of Luther Craven staring at the ceiling with blank eyes.

"Leo?"

Leo looked up surprised to find Charlie watching him.

With wide eyes, Charlie whispered, "Will I be arrested for killing him?"

Leo stood up with a smile. He approached her.

Charlie stared at the man she had killed.

Leo wiped wet hair out of her eyes. "No, sweetie. This was clearly self-defense. You were protecting yourself. You had no choice."

Turning back to the crime scene, Leo scanned the signs of a struggle. He spotted a red blinking light from a shelf of knick-knacks above the sink.

Leo stepped closer to the sink. He reached up to pull down a small black object. He shook his head. "Plus, it looks like the whole thing was recorded."

Leo turned the mini-camera off. He placed it on the kitchen table then returned to Charlie. Frowning at her horrified expression, he pulled her into another hug. She would be haunted by the invasion of her privacy for a long time. *How long has Cavanaugh been watching her? Has he been watching all of us?*

D'Angelo Walker squeezed his eyes shut hopeful the bullet would be for him. He tried to ignore the great noise his family made as they shouted for Cavanaugh's henchmen to stop their deadly game.

The hammer was cocked with a loud click. D'Angelo waited for the explosive boom that would end his life and free his family from the Russian roulette game.

Silence. D'Angelo grimaced at the lack of sounds. What was taking Remington so long to pull the trigger? Maybe this was part of the twisted game.

"Sorry to interrupt your game, Walkers."

D'Angelo's eyes flew open at the familiar voice. He stared at Frankie pointing her own weapon at Remington's head. He glanced around the basement. Other police officers arrested Cavanaugh's henchmen.

As Remington was passed off to another cop, the Walkers were freed from their bonds.

D'Angelo limped toward his family. He wrapped his arms around Big Mama as she sobbed. His brothers joined the family hug. *Thank You, Jesus!*

Frankie said, "I don't know if you want to know, D'Angelo, but the bullet was in your chamber."

Nodding, D'Angelo sniffed attempting to control his emotions. He lowered his head with closed eyes. *Good. It would have killed me to have one of the others die.*

"Why did you come to our house, Lemmons?" D'Angelo asked.

Frankie shrugged, "I figured Charlie has Leo and Mags has Weldon. You're the ones I figured could use the back-up."

Big Mama approached Frankie. She wrapped her skinny arms around her.

Frankie patted her on the back awkwardly with wide eyes.

D'Angelo beamed at her reaction to a Big Mama hug. *She's not used to such affection.*

Big Mama cackled, "Thank you, honey. We most certainly needed the back-up."

Charlotte Pearl sat on her sofa. The police had entered her apartment. They were taking statements and examining the crime scene. The detective in charge told her no charges would be filed against her. *That's a relief.*

"Thank you, Detective Morris."

Charlotte smiled weakly.

Leo sat down next to her.

Charlotte surrendered her hand to him. She leaned her head on his shoulder.

Rubbing her hand, Leo kissed her on the head.

Charlotte longed to be at peace about the events of the evening. However, nagging questions plagued her. "Leo, why did he try to kill me? Obviously, he was working for Peter Cavanaugh, but why does he always pick me?"

"It wasn't just you, Charlie. Peter Cavanaugh's playing a game of fear. He wanted us to face our fears tonight in his own sick and twisted way," explained Leo.

Charlotte sat up straighter. It made sense now. "That's why Craven tried to drown me. That's my greatest fear. But what about you? You were kidnapped for a while, but not hurt."

Leo nodded, "True. He knew my greatest fear is losing you. Thank God they failed to make me face that one!"

Charlotte leaned forward to kiss him. She closed her eyes cherishing the connection as his mouth touched hers. She wrapped her arms around his neck.

As the kiss ended, the couple remained close staring at each other both obviously thankful to still have each other. Charlotte moved her hands to his shoulders. *Peter Cavanaugh is a monster. He threatens us with what we fear most.*

Charlotte leaned back as horror covered her.

Leo asked, "Charlie? What's wrong?"

"What about Mags?" cried Charlotte.

Leo's eyes widened at the question. His shoulders tensed under her hands. "Fire."

Charlotte released Leo. She grabbed her cell phone and clicked on Mags' cell number. She growled under her breath as the call went straight to voicemail. "She's not answering her cell. I'll try her house."

Charlotte dialed the other phone number she had for Mags. She sighed in relief as the call was answered.

"Hello?"

"Gloria. It's Charlie."

"Hi, Ms. Charlotte. Are you looking for Ms. Magnolia?"

Charlotte swallowed hard. Hope filled her at the chance to talk to Mags. "Yes, honey."

"Well, she went to the art museum with Mr. Weldon. He surprised her with it," replied Gloria.

"Great. Bye, Gloria."

As she ended the call, Charlotte stood up.

Leo already had his car keys in his hand.

Charlotte explained, "Weldon took her to the art museum."

"Let's go."

Detective Frankie Lemmons sighed in relief. She stared at Leo's number on the screen of her cell phone. She clicked on the accept icon and placed the phone at her ear. "Hey, Knight."

"Lemmons, you need to check on the Walkers for me."

Frankie rolled her eyes. "Your timing could use some work, Knight. I'm with them now. Remington Holland along with some other dirtbags have been arrested for trying to kill them in a game of Russian roulette."

"Is anyone hurt?" demanded Leo.

Frankie snorted, "Relax, Knight. They're fine. Now, Big Mama is making me eat some of her famous chocolate chip cookies. You okay?"

"Yes. I was kidnapped and Charlie was almost drowned, but we are both safe now. I'll fill you in more later. Charlie and I are going to check in on Mags and Weldon. Gloria said they went to the art museum," explained Leo.

Frankie asked, "Do you want me to meet you there?"

"No. We've got Weldon as back-up. Stay with the Walkers in case Cavanaugh tries something else."

"Okay. Be careful, Knight. This thing isn't over yet."

CHAPTER 14

ONGOING OPPRESSION

Gloria Fairbanks tilted her head at D'Quan's number appearing on the screen of her cell phone. She was not sure she wanted to talk to her ex-boyfriend. Deep down she hoped he would apologize, so they could make amends. Gloria accepted the call with hope rising inside her.   "Hello?"

"Gloria, are you okay?"

Gloria frowned at D'Quan's frightened voice. "What's going on?"

"Some gunmen came to our house and tried to kill us. Detective Lemmons saved us. I wanted to make sure you're safe. Detective Knight and Ms. Charlotte are checking on Ms. Magnolia and Mr. Weldon."

Gloria swallowed hard at the news her family and friends were in danger. She opened her mouth to assert she was safe. However, a loud bang on the door downstairs changed her mind.

Gloria jumped up from her bed. She opened her door to listen for any sounds.

"Gloria?"

Gloria shushed D'Quan as he waited on the other end of the line. She listened hard.

Heavy footsteps were slowly coming up the stairs. Closing her door and locking it, Gloria scanned her room for a solution to her problem.

"Gloria?"

Gloria whispered, "There's someone in the house."

"You have to hide, Gloria. Hurry!"

Nodding, Gloria placed her connected cell phone in her pink robe pocket. She headed into her closet. Closing the door, she sat on the floor. She prayed the intruder would not be able to find her. *Please, God. I don't want to die.*

Detective Leo Knight and Charlie raced up the art museum stairs. When they reached the door, it was locked.

Leo slammed a fist on the glass alerting the security guard who hurried over with wide eyes. "Detective Knight. We need to see someone inside."

The security guard stammered as he moved to the side. "There's no one here, Detective. Everyone has gone home for the night."

Leo frowned at the news. *Then where are Mags and Weldon?*

"Weldon!"

Leo turned in the direction Charlie was running.

Weldon Hitchcock waited outside of the men's restroom.

Leo yelled, "Where's Mags?"

"The glow in the dark exhibit. What's wrong?"

Charlie replied, "Peter Cavanaugh."

Weldon's eyes grew wide at the news. "It's this way."

The three adults began to cross the lobby of the art museum toward one of the hallways. Leo gritted his teeth. *Please let her be okay, Lord.*

Suddenly, a loud ringing echoed through the museum. It was the fire alarm. Leo ran faster leaving Weldon and Charlie following behind. *Fire!*

Magnolia Ruby cowered in the corner on the floor. She coughed at the thick smoke filling the closet area. She closed her eyes. She was going to die like her family did so long ago. *Please, Lord, make it quick and painless.*

Suddenly, a loud crash knocked the door open. Her eyes snapped open as light streamed into the closet. Flickering flames danced around the open doorway. Magnolia stood up leaning her back on the wall fearing the advancing flames.

"Mags!"

Leo leapt through the flames toward her. "Come on, Mags. I've got you."

With wide eyes, Magnolia shook her head and shoved her hands against him. "No! I can't!"

"We have to leave now, Mags, before it gets worse. Come on."

"No!"

Swallowing the desperation rising inside him, Detective Leo Knight stared at Mags as she refused to leave the closet with him. He flicked his gaze toward the fire. It grew by the minute. *We won't be able to get out soon.*

"Leo, carry her!"

Charlie's frantic voice drove Leo into action. He turned back to Mags. She shook uncontrollably.

Leo grabbed her and picked her up in his arms. He ignored her screams as he tightened his grip to keep hold of her in her struggles.

Taking a deep breath, Leo leapt through the growing flames. He prayed neither of them would get burned. He landed on his feet on the other side of the fierce fire with Mags safely in his arms.

Leo staggered down the hallway where Weldon and Charlie were waiting.

As they exited the art museum, Leo slowed down on the stairs so not to trip injuring Mags or himself. They reached the bottom of the stairs and moved to the sidewalk.

The sirens of firetrucks filled the air as the massive red vehicles pulled up to the art museum.

Leo set Mags down on the sidewalk gently.

Charlie knelt beside their friend.

Leo turned toward the firetrucks. A police car pulled up next to them. "I need to talk to that cop. I'll be right back."

Racing over, Leo waved a hand to flag down the police officers as they exited their vehicle.

Charlotte Pearl brushed silver strands of hair out of Mags' eyes with her hand. She shushed her trying to calm her down. Mags' hysteria began to die down. "You're safe, Mags. God protected all of us tonight. He's been faithful. Just breathe, Mags. You're safe. We're all safe."

Charlotte smiled weakly as the tension left Mags' body and calm returned to her. She glanced over at Leo. He was clearly explaining what had happened to the police officers.

Charlotte looked over at Weldon. He paced back and forth talking on his cell phone. She narrowed her eyes at Mags' boyfriend annoyed he was not comforting his girlfriend. *Something's wrong here. Leo would be focused on me not his cell phone. Is he a part of all this?*

Weldon Hitchcock waited for Peter Cavanaugh to answer his phone so he could report the results of his part of the game.

"Well?"

Weldon winced at Peter's harsh tone. He could tell the boss was already irritated. "She's alive, boss. She got out of the fire."

"That seems to be the theme of the night," snorted Peter.

Weldon asked, "What do you mean?"

"The Walkers are alive. Charlie is alive and killed Craven. Leo didn't lose Charlie. Now, Magnolia is alive. I would say this round goes to the Jewels of Intrigue," explained Peter.

Weldon bit his lip at the fury clear in Peter's voice. "What do we do now?"

"Come back to rendezvous. We need to plan for the next round of the game."

"Be right there, boss."

As the call ended, Weldon shook his head. He tromped over to the spot where Nolia and Charlie were sitting on the sidewalk. He smiled warmly at the women as they looked up at him.

Charlie asked, "Everything okay?"

"No. I'm needed for a case."

Weldon focused on Nolia. "I'm sorry, Nolia. I have to go, but I'll be back soon to check on you."

"I understand. Be safe," Nolia said with a weak smile.

"I will."

Weldon spun around. He marched toward his car. He was not looking forward to the lecture he was sure would come from their angry boss.

As her bedroom door crashed open, Gloria Fairbanks slapped her hands over her mouth to stop a scream. She held her breath staring at the closet door. She expected it to be opened any second.

Gloria swallowed her fear. Her mind reeled with her options. *There's no way out. Maybe I have something I can use to defend myself, but what?*

"I'm going to find you, kid. Why don't you come out and quit wasting time?"

Gloria shook her head. She glanced around in the dark for anything she could use to defend herself. Her hand touched the loop end of her tennis racket. She moved her hands to the handle gripping it tightly ready to hit anyone who entered her closet.

Gloria stared at the bottom of the door where light shone in. Shadows stopped in front of the crack of light. She suppressed a whimper. A tear escaped and rolled down her cheek. Her heart pounded as her mind raced with a prayer. *Please, Lord, scare him away. Protect me from danger.*

CHAPTER 15

PROSPECTIVE PLAN

Lying on the ambulance gurney, Magnolia Ruby waited as patiently as she could. The paramedics checked her for injuries and smoke inhalation. She took a deep breath as instructed feeling shaky but thankful to be alive.

Magnolia glanced over at Charlie and Leo standing nearby ready to give her more comfort. She smiled weakly at them reassuring them she was calm once more. *Thank You, Lord, for getting them to me in time. You kept us all safe tonight.*

"We need to take you to the hospital, ma'am. Just breathe slowly."

Magnolia obeyed the paramedics as they placed an oxygen mask over her nose and mouth. She wanted to protest. However, the fire had shaken her up. Her body was exhausted from inhaling the smoke. Her heart began to pound again as she pictured how the fire could have destroyed her. *Stop it, Mags. You're safe.*

Magnolia closed her eyes to calm her nerves. She took another deep breath wishing to sleep the nightmare away.

Suddenly, her eyes snapped open in shock.

"Gloria!"

Gloria Fairbanks squeezed her eyes tightly. Her closet door opened. She swung the tennis racket hoping to hit her attacker. However, she refused to look at him in the face. If she could not identify him, then she might be allowed to live.

Gloria screamed as the racket was snatched out of her hands.

Strong arms wrapped around her. Gloria punched her fists at the intruder.

"It's okay. You're safe, Little Miss."

Her eyes snapped open in surprise at the familiar voice. She stared at D'Angelo. He held her comfortingly.

Sobbing, Gloria hugged him back. She buried her face against his shoulder thankful to be alive. *Thank You, Lord!*

"Are you okay?"

Gloria turned her head to peer out of the closet. She smiled weakly at Frankie handcuffing a man on the carpet. She nodded wiping tears from her face.

Gloria gasped. D'Quan was still connected on her phone. She pulled it out of her robe pocket. She raised it to her ear. "D'Quan, I'm okay. Frankie and D'Angelo are here. I'm safe."

A loud sigh came from the other end of the phone. "Great! I'm glad you're okay."

Gloria smiled at the relief in his voice.

"Gloria, I love you," D'Quan said.

Her eyes widened at the sentiment. She glanced at D'Angelo. He knelt close enough to her to have heard what D'Quan said.

D'Angelo smirked, "Well, don't look at me. I didn't say it, Little Miss."

Gloria stood up and moved to the corner away from him.

D'Angelo chuckled as he left the closet.

"You do?" asked Gloria.

"Yes. I love you, Gloria."

"I love you too, D'Quan."

A whoop of joy echoed from outside her closet. Gloria rolled her eyes. She exited it raising her eyebrows at D'Angelo. He slapped a hand over his mouth with a shrug.

Gloria said, "I'll see you soon, D'Quan."

As the couple ended their call, Gloria walked over to her bed. She sank down. The frightening moment had drained her into exhaustion. Her emotions had taken her on quite a roller coaster ride.

D'Angelo sat down beside her. He placed a comforting arm around her shoulder.

Gloria leaned against him with a sigh.

D'Angelo said, "It's okay, Little Miss. No one is going to hurt you as long as I'm around."

"Oh, really? You wouldn't even tell me you love me," teased Gloria.

D'Angelo shrugged, "What's to tell? You know you're my angel."

Gloria beamed at the loving sentiment.

D'Angelo placed a gentle kiss on her head.

Gloria giggled, "You're not so bad yourself, Big D."

Lying in a hospital bed, Magnolia Ruby ended her phone call with Gloria. She thanked God for keeping her daughter safe from the danger Peter Cavanaugh had sent her way. "Gloria is safe. D'Angelo and Frankie reached the house in time to arrest a man sent by Cavanaugh."

Charlie smiled warmly, "Thank God! Where is she now?"

"D'Angelo took her back to his house for the night."

Leo nodded, "Good idea. I have a police car watching the Walker house until we find Cavanaugh. They'll be safe this time."

Magnolia set her cell phone on the table beside her hospital bed. She folded her hands feeling able to relax now.

"Oh, man," mumbled Leo.

Magnolia asked, "What's wrong?"

"Nothing. I forgot about my parents. I have ten missed calls from my mother. I'm sure she is ticked. I'll be back," explained Leo.

Magnolia observed Charlie sitting down in a chair beside the bed.

Charlie averted her gaze to the television hanging on the wall.

Magnolia watched her for a few minutes. She could tell something was wrong. It had to have something to do with Leo's parents. That was when Charlie's mood changed. "So, how do you feel about meeting Leo's parents, Charlie?"

Charlie remained silent changing channels.

Magnolia was about to ask again.

Switching the television off, Charlie turned toward her. "I'm scared. I know it is silly to be afraid to meet his parents when we have all just been near death, but I am. What if they don't like me? What if they turn Leo against me? What if they ruin everything?"

Magnolia interrupted, "What if they like you and your relationship with Leo? What if you gain a family?"

"That's my prayer, Mags, but you and I both know things don't always turn out the way we want."

Magnolia nodded, "True, but God has a plan for all of us. Trust Him to do what's best with your life. I'll be praying too, Charlie."

"Thanks, Mags."

Movement drew their attention to the open doorway. Frankie entered the room with a foam take-out box in her hands. She nodded toward them then sat down in another chair.

Magnolia smiled warmly, "Thank you for saving Gloria, Frankie. I am truly grateful for you."

"No big deal. She's a nice kid."

Frankie opened the box to reveal a cheeseburger with a piece of apple pie under the top bun.

Magnolia shook her head at the odd concoction. She had witnessed Frankie eating it once. *The famous Frankie pie sandwich.*

Frankie took a large bite out of the pie sandwich.

Leo reentered the room. "My parents are heading home early. They'll try to visit with us another time."

"Okay," Charlie said.

Magnolia smirked at the return of Charlie's smile. Not having to meet Leo's parents yet seemed to have brightened her mood.

Leo turned his attention to his partner.

Frankie stared back at him evenly.

Leo asked, "Didn't you already have one of those today, Lemmons?"

"Back off, Knight. I'm a little stressed," grunted Frankie taking a bigger bite.

Magnolia nodded. They were all stressed to their limit after the events of the evening. *If only it was over.*

Detective Frankie Lemmons savored the sweet pie and the meaty burger as the flavors blasted her taste buds. Her body relaxed as the familiar therapy worked.

"What do you have to be stressed about, Lemmons?" Leo asked.

Recalling no one knew what had happened to her except Alice, Frankie mumbled, "I was locked in my car trunk."

"What? When? How did you get out?"

Holding up a hand, Frankie said, "Relax, Knight. I'm fine. I left here and two goons threw me into the trunk. I panicked since I hate tight spaces, but Ms. Alice saved me. Then I headed to the Walkers' house and rescued them. No big deal."

"It is a really big deal. Nobody messes with my partner," snapped Leo.

Rolling her eyes, Frankie said, "You are so sentimental, Knight."

Frankie lowered her head. She picked up her pie sandwich to hide her smile. It pleased her to hear Leo so protective of her. *I feel the same. Someone messes with Leopha and I'll kick his butt.*

Frankie said, "So, Knight. You said you were kidnapped. What happened?"

"I was leaving the station, and someone placed a chloroform cloth on my face. I woke up in a warehouse. Simmons, the prison guard, kept me captive until he received a text Charlie was dead," explained Leo.

Frankie glanced over at Charlie. Why would someone send an untrue text? "Who sent the text?"

Charlie shrugged, "I did."

Leo turned his head to his girlfriend. "I didn't know that. Why would you send a text you were dead?"

"Because I didn't want anyone else to come to my apartment to kill me," Charlie said.

Frankie frowned, "So what did happen at your apartment, Charlie?"

"I was washing dishes when Luther Craven grabbed me and tried to drown me in the sink," explained Charlie.

Frankie grunted, "Huh. I knew washing dishes was dangerous."

Charlie smiled at Frankie's attempt to lighten the mood. "I always thought so too. Anyway, I stabbed him with a meat thermometer in the neck."

Frankie groaned, "Ouch. That will get it done."

"It's not funny, Lemmons," muttered Leo.

Frankie snorted, "Lighten up, Knight. We could use a little humor now. What about you, Mags? What did Cavanaugh plan for you?"

Mags said, "Weldon took me to the art museum. There is a glow in the dark exhibit in a closet-like room. I went in and then found I was locked in. Someone started a fire and Leo saved me from being barbecued."

Frankie smirked at Mags' own use of humor to help the grim situation.

Mags added, "I think Weldon did it."

Magnolia Ruby waited patiently for the others to react to her accusation. She had debated about whether or not to tell them her suspicions. There was no real proof. She only had a hunch.

Leo asked, "Why do you think that?"

"The note found at Felicia's apartment said she didn't deserve to be a mother. I had mentioned the same thing to Weldon when we saw her at the grocery store," explained Magnolia.

Frankie tilted her head to the side. "That doesn't mean he is working for Peter Cavanaugh."

"Well, he and Gloria were the only ones who knew I was at the art museum. He suggested I go first into the glow in the dark exhibit Then the door was locked. Weldon just happened to be away when the fire started and I was trapped," Magnolia said.

Charlie added, "Plus, he was on the phone instead of comforting you which seems like an unnatural reaction. Then he had to leave for a case at night? It seems fishy to me too."

Magnolia nodded in agreement. She watched the two police detectives absorb the facts.

Leo shrugged, "He could be involved."

"We should bring him in and question him," Frankie added.

Shaking her head, Magnolia said, "I don't think that's a good idea."

"Why not?" asked Charlie.

Magnolia said, "I think Weldon could be the key to bringing down Peter Cavanaugh, but he won't be any good to us locked up."

Silence. Magnolia waited for her friends to ask her for her plan. She had been thinking about it since she had settled in her hospital room. She hoped they would go along with it.

Leo sighed, "Okay. What do you want to do?"

"Change the game."

Glaring, Peter Cavanaugh sat at the head of his table. The henchmen stared anxiously at him. He scanned the men who had returned from the failed game. *Weldon, Krupin, Simmons, and Duffy. That's all who escaped the police?*

Peter listened as each man recounted their part of the game and how their victims were still alive. He liked that Simmons had been able to fulfill his section of the plan by kidnapping Detective Knight though Craven had failed to kill Charlie which would have devastated the police detective. *I knew that coward shouldn't have been involved. He was too weak to even drown a woman.*

"Boss!"

Peter glanced up.

Terrence Morris strutted into the room.

Peter waited for him to sit down and explain his tardiness.

Morris said, "I was able to examine Charlie's apartment. She killed Craven with a meat thermometer."

Weldon snorted, "How?"

"Stabbed it into his neck," replied Morris.

Simmons asked, "Did you find out anything else?"

Peter returned his gaze to the table waiting for Morris to answer. He had not heard anything about the attack on Gloria. He had texted Morris to find out the result of that stage of the game.

Morris said, "Yeah. I heard on the police scanner Paxton was arrested at Ruby's house. The girl's alive and well."

Peter slammed his fist on the wooden table drawing the attention from his henchmen. His silence would scare the men more than an outburst. He reflected on what the next step of his game could be to give him victorious results. *I need a more drastic approach if I am going to win.*

Raising his head to glare at his men, Peter said, "Weldon, find a way to bring Magnolia to me at the warehouse tomorrow night. The rest of you meet me there at eight o'clock sharp. I want no more mistakes." *This game is far from over.*

CHAPTER 16

QUESTIONABLE QUEST

Magnolia Ruby waved at Lucretia Cushings as Gloria's aunt drove into the driveway. She turned back toward the living room with a smile.

"Gloria, Lucretia is here. Don't forget your suitcase."

Gloria trudged toward the door with her backpack on her back and her suitcase in her hand.

Magnolia smiled warmly, "Don't worry, honey. This will only be for a few days. I want to make sure you are safe while we finish this case."

"I know, Ms. Magnolia, but I want you to be safe too," mumbled Gloria.

"I'll be fine, sweetheart."

Magnolia hugged her daughter planting a tender kiss on the side of her head. "I'll call you tonight. Have a good day at school. I love you, Gloria."

"I love you too, Ms. Magnolia."

Magnolia watched as Gloria climbed into her aunt's car. She hated to be away from her even for a few days. The duo drove away. *We have to stop Cavanaugh. Then our family will be safe.*

Weldon Hitchcock groaned as the clock reached seven o'clock. He had spent the entire day trying to come up with a plan to get Nolia to go with him to the warehouse. All his ideas sounded stupid especially since her near death experience from the previous night.

Weldon picked up his cell phone as it began to ring. He smirked at the caller. *Nolia.*

"Hello?"

"Hello, Weldon. I hadn't heard from you and I was getting worried."

Weldon replied, "I'm sorry, Nolia. I didn't mean to worry you. How are you feeling?"

"Better. I was wondering if you could come over," Nolia said.

"Of course. What time would you like me?"

Nolia answered, "As soon as possible would be great."

Weldon paused at the urgency. "Is something wrong?" *Does she know?*

Nolia replied, "No. I need your help."

"With what?"

"I'll tell you when you get here," Nolia said.

As the couple ended the call, Weldon grabbed his car keys eager to see what Nolia wanted from him. His mind raced with ideas of how he could convince her to go with him to the warehouse. *It will have to be convincing. She's so sharp.*

Magnolia Ruby sat on her couch waiting for Weldon to arrive. Her plan rolled through her mind. She longed to end the nightmare that had been affecting the group for months. Opening her purse, she spied the Glock she had bought and trained with at the shooting range months ago when she thought Peter Cavanaugh had killed Charlie.

A loud knock came to the front door. Magnolia raised her eyebrows as she stood to answer it. *That was fast. He must be eager to help his boss.*

Magnolia opened the door pasting on a smile. "Weldon, you got here fast."

"Well, when my woman wants my help, I don't waste any time getting to her," Weldon said.

Magnolia braced herself. He kissed her on the lips. She suppressed the cringe threatening to shake her body at how easily Weldon played the part of the trustworthy boyfriend. *He's been deceiving me for months.*

"What can I help you with, dear?"

Magnolia said, "I wanted you to come with me to Dana and Peter Calvin's apartment."

"Why?"

"I want to find something to use against Peter Cavanaugh."

Weldon nodded, "Okay. Let's go. I'll drive."

Magnolia pasted on a smile. She carried her purse out of the house as she followed him. *So willing to help your boss, are we?*

Detective Leo Knight drove his unmarked police car following Weldon's vehicle. He kept his distance not wanting the traitor to see he was behind him. He hated Mags was alone in the car with their suspect though he knew she was armed.

Frankie said, "He turned the wrong way."

Leo glanced at Frankie who was checking her GPS on her phone. "What?"

"He was supposed to go straight to get to the Calvins' apartment," Frankie explained.

Leo cringed at the change in directions. "Do you think he is on to us?"

Frankie shook her head. "No."

"Then why would he go the wrong way?"

Frankie muttered, "Maybe he is taking us to Peter Cavanaugh himself."

Peter Cavanaugh sat on a wooden staircase at the end of the warehouse. His henchmen finished moving crates to create a maze for the final round of his game. He glanced toward a large glass window as light came into the room. Weldon's car parked in the warehouse parking lot. He lightly clapped his hands as he saw a woman sitting in the passenger seat. *He got Magnolia to come.*

"Okay, boys. Spread out and be ready." *It's time to win the game.*

Magnolia Ruby frowned at Weldon. She pretended she did not understand why he was stopping at the warehouse. "Where are we?"

"This warehouse belongs to Cavanaugh. We will find something here to use against him," explained Weldon.

Magnolia asked, "How do you know?"

"I've done my research."

Magnolia nodded. *And I've done mine, Mr. Hitchcock.*

Magnolia climbed out of the deceitful man's car staring at the towering warehouse. Was it the same one where Simmons had kept Leo while Craven attacked Charlie? She followed Weldon to an unlocked door. *This is where the game ends.*

As they entered the warehouse, Weldon Hitchcock pulled his revolver from his holster. It had been his first weapon as a cop years ago. He hoped it would not the last time he used it. It had been a trusty gun throughout his police career.

Cavanaugh's text had said to bring Nolia inside then shoot her. Weldon regretted how he had deceived her for many months. He wished things had been different. "I'm sorry, Nolia."

"For what?"

Weldon frowned at the odd sound of her voice. He spun around with his gun ready. He glared at the floor where a cell phone sat with a lit-up screen. He picked it up confused. "Nolia?"

Nolia said, "I want to thank you for bringing us to Peter Cavanaugh, Weldon, but I'm afraid I'm breaking up with you."

As the call ended, Weldon cursed under his breath. He scanned the shadows trying to figure out which way she went. He stepped into the darkness with his revolver pointing the way. *I must find her.*

Smirking, Peter Cavanaugh watched the scene below with great interest.

Magnolia pulled her own weapon from her purse. She moved behind some crates.

Weldon spun around before picking up the phone. Peter rolled his eyes. *She tricked you, idiot.*

Weldon began to hunt for his prey.

Peter shook his head. He knew exactly how the final round of the game would end. *I wonder if the detectives have arrived yet.*

Detective Leo Knight entered through a side door of the warehouse. It was the same place Simmons had kept him during his kidnapping experience. He held his Glock ready hoping Mags hadn't strayed too far with Weldon Hitchcock.

Leo turned toward his partner.

Frankie had her own weapon ready.

The two police detectives began to creep through the shadows searching for Cavanaugh and his minions.

The crates had been placed in a way that seemed more like a maze than a warehouse.

Leo suppressed a snort. Staying silent was crucial in his game. *Of course, he has a maze to make his game more exciting.*

Frankie motioned to get Leo's attention. She pointed down one of the tunnels.

Duffy was standing with his back to them.

Leo nodded. He pointed down another tunnel.

Krupin stood smoking a cigarette with his gun in his other hand.

The two detectives nodded ready for the showdown. They moved behind a large forklift that had been left to the side. They prepared to arrest the two henchmen.

Frankie barked, "Police! Drop your weapons!"

Leo's eyes widened.

Krupin and Duffy spun around firing their guns.

The detectives were able to safely return fire from their position behind the machine. Both minions moved behind the crates to shield themselves from the attack.

Gunfire suddenly rang out in the warehouse. Magnolia Ruby bit back a gasp. She glanced around to make sure no one was sneaking up on her. Then she stepped in a different direction with her Glock ready in case she met Peter Cavanaugh or one of his minions. *Lord, please keep Leo and Frankie safe.*

Suddenly, a shuffling noise came from behind her. Magnolia slid into the shadows.

Weldon came into view. He moved past her.

Magnolia was tempted to shoot him, but it would not be self-defense. *I'm not a killer.*

Magnolia peered out of the shadows.

Weldon went down another crate tunnel.

Magnolia turned her gaze the other way. Her eyes widened.

Peter Cavanaugh sat on a wooden staircase watching the action as if he was at a baseball game. He had caused so much trouble.

Magnolia marched toward the open area leaving the safety of the crates.

"Nolia!"

A great shove knocked Magnolia to the concrete floor. She winced at a gunshot closer than any of the others had been.

Magnolia used her hands to turn over onto her rear end. She stared with wide eyes at Weldon standing above her with a revolver in his hand. Where had the bullet gone?

Magnolia glanced over. A dead man laid on the floor.

Weldon hissed, "Come on, Nolia. Get out of sight."

Weldon offered a hand to her.

Magnolia took it in her confusion.

Weldon helped her to her feet. He pulled her toward the crate maze once more.

Suddenly, a gunshot rang out. Magnolia screamed.

Cursing, Weldon fell to the concrete ground.

Magnolia spun around. Peter blew the smoke from the tip of his Glock like he was in an old movie. She glared at the heinous man as he smirked at her.

"Mags!"

Magnolia turned back.

Charlie rushed over to where Weldon had fallen.

Moving to her side, Magnolia gasped, "Charlie, what are you doing here?"

"Helping my friends of course," answered Charlie.

Magnolia nodded, "Thanks. Speaking of friends, Weldon, what in the world is going on?"

"I'll explain later. Right now, we need to be careful. Cavanaugh's got more men around here," Weldon said.

Charlie placed her hands onto his bleeding shoulder putting pressure on the wound.

Magnolia flicked her gaze to the stairs.

Peter Cavanaugh applauded with a smile.

Magnolia said, "Stay with him, Charlie."

"Mags."

Narrowing her eyes at Peter, Magnolia mumbled, "I promised to finish this and I always keep my promises." *The final showdown will be between him and me.*

CHAPTER 17

ROOFTOP REVEAL

Detective Leo Knight sighed in relief. One of his bullets hit Krupin in the chest ending the henchman's fight. He spun to the other side eager to assist Frankie with Duffy.

"I give up! I surrender!" Duffy shouted.

Leo barked, "Drop the gun, Duffy, and put your hands into the air."

Duffy dropped the weapon to the ground with a clunk. His hands flew into the air.

Frankie rushed forward. She pulled out a set of handcuffs. She roughly turned Duffy around arresting him with a smirk of satisfaction on her face.

Leo scanned the warehouse.

Peter Cavanaugh ran up a wooden staircase.

Mags followed him with her Glock in her hand.

Leo moved forward to help his friend stop the psychopath who had tormented the group for months.

Suddenly, a gunshot popped in the air. Leo spun around with his Glock ready.

Frankie pointed her weapon upward.

Leo snapped his gaze in the same direction in time to see Simmons falling from a tall tower of crates. The prison guard landed with a thud on the concrete floor.

Frankie smirked, "Didn't your mother ever tell you to watch where you're going, Leopha?"

"Funny, Francesca."

Leo's eyes widened. He slapped a hand onto his forehead. "Oh, no! My mother!"

Frankie frowned, "What?"

"I was supposed to call her," Leo said.

"Tell her it's your girlfriend's fault."

Leo spun in the direction of the familiar voice.

Charlie helped Weldon walk toward them. He had an arm around her shoulder.

Leo rushed forward. He helped Charlie with the man they all considered a traitor. "Charlie, what are you doing here?"

"Helping my friends of course," Charlie said with a smile.

"I told you to stay at the diner."

Frankie snorted, "Careful, Knight. Women don't like to be told what to do."

Leo opened his mouth with a retort. He glanced back at the stairs. Peter was no longer visible. Mags had reached the top.

Leo said, "Never mind. We can debate it later. I have to help Mags." *It's not too late.*

Magnolia Ruby climbed up the creaky wooden staircase. At the top was a red door marked ROOF. She was not sure it was a good idea to follow the sinister man onto the rooftop. However, she wanted to end his games for good.

Magnolia opened the red door with her Glock in hand. She stepped out into the night wincing at the dim moonlight. Scanning the rooftop, she aimed her gun in case the psychopath jumped out of the shadows at her.

"Over here, Magnolia."

Magnolia snapped her gaze to the far end of the rooftop.

Peter Cavanaugh stood with his arms crossed.

Magnolia snapped, "It's over, Peter."

"I know."

Magnolia clutched her Glock tighter. She had to be careful listening to the manipulator. He always had a new trick. *What's his game now?*

Charlotte Pearl bit her lip. Paramedics helped Weldon onto a gurney before rolling him away. She moved her attention to Duffy being led away by police officers. They had arrived to provide back-up.

Charlotte averted her gaze from the three men who had been killed in the warehouse. She was thankful none of them were her friends.

Charlotte stared at the wooden staircase with her heart pounding. Mags and Leo had not returned from chasing Peter Cavanaugh. She shivered at what could happen to her friends as they faced the psychopath. *Please help Mags and Leo come back to me safely, Lord.*

Staring up at the stars, Peter Cavanaugh took a deep breath of fresh air. "It is a beautiful night, isn't it, Magnolia?"

Silence. Peter glanced down watching her.

Magnolia stepped across the rooftop toward him with her Glock ready.

Peter stared calmly at her. Would she have had the guts to shoot him? *We will never know.*

Peter said, "My father was a cruel man. He hated me because I was a wimpy child with asthma and chronic fears. My father believed if you faced your fears dramatically, then you wouldn't have them anymore."

Peter turned toward the edge of the roof. He stared down at the city with its twinkling lights and busy streets. "I was terrified of heights, so my father decided to help me face my fear by shoving me off the high diving board. It didn't work. It only made me more frightened. My grandfather was furious at him, but of course, my father wasn't sorry. He never was sorry. Well, I guess he was when he died."

Peter spun back to Magnolia pleased to see she was listening to his rant with clear interest. "I helped my father face his own fear when I was in college. He had a great fear of spiders so I made sure he died by a venomous one. Of course, I read it in a book once."

Magnolia Ruby swallowed the bile rising in her throat. She could not believe Peter Cavanaugh talked about murdering his father as if it was a common normal occurrence. She kept her Glock pointed at him not trusting him enough to lower the weapon.

Peter sighed, "You are such a worthy opponent, Magnolia."

Magnolia touched the trigger with her finger. "Surrender or die, Peter."

Peter said, "I'm so amazed by your ability to survive horrors and win games against me. You actually stunned me to the point I had to plan this last game. It's not as complex as the others since I had to make it quickly after yesterday's failure."

Magnolia glared at his long, drawn-out speech. "Don't make me shoot you, Peter. Surrender."

Peter saluted her by placing his open hand to his forehead.

"I hereby surrender my title of Game King to the Queen of Games. May you keep the title for many years as you weave deceptive games among the masses. Farewell, Queen Magnolia."

Magnolia stared at him. What was he saying? Her eyes widened.

Peter Cavanaugh spun around. He jumped off the warehouse roof.

Magnolia gasped. Horror covered her at his suicide. *Why would he do that?*

Detective Leo Knight stopped at an open red door with the word ROOF written on it. He held his Glock ready and advanced onto the rooftop. He scanned the area then froze.

Mags stood at the far end of the rooftop.

Leo hurried forward. He glanced around to make sure Peter Cavanaugh or his henchmen were not hiding in the shadows holding his friend hostage as bait to lure him to them. "Where's Cavanaugh?"

Mags turned toward him. Her horrified expression startled him.

"Mags?"

Mags mumbled, "He jumped."

Leo frowned at the unexpected news. He marched over to the edge of the rooftop. He expected to see some way of escape Cavanaugh had found. He peered over the edge.

Peter Cavanaugh's body laid crumpled on the ground below.

Leo closed his eyes with a satisfied sigh. His friends were finally safe.

"Leo?"

Leo's eyes snapped open. He turned back to Mags.

"Game over."

CHAPTER 18

SWEET SOCIAL

Staring at the hospital room door, Magnolia Ruby debated about whether or not she should go in. Taking a deep breath, she knocked a fist on the door.

"Come in."

Opening the door, Magnolia entered the hospital room. Her eyes fell on Weldon. He sat up in his bed.

"Hello, Nolia."

Magnolia placed her hands on her hips. "You owe me an explanation, Weldon."

Weldon gestured to a chair beside his bed. "You're right, Nolia." Magnolia sat down in the chair.

Weldon explained, "Peter Cavanaugh was right about one thing. I was an Undercover Underdog, but I was undercover against him."

Magnolia crossed her arms. "How did you get in his crew?"

"Peter came to me after our case at Cloud Nine. He said he knew you and wanted to know about our relationship. I could tell there was something off about him. You don't serve as a cop as long as I did without getting a feeling about people. When he asked if I would be willing to help him play a game with you, I decided the best way to keep an eye on him and protect you was to join him," explained Weldon.

Magnolia's temper flared. Her mind recalled all the group had experienced during Peter's games. She narrowed her eyes at him.

Weldon had known the psychopath's plans without telling any of the friends.

Magnolia asked, "So, you knew he kidnapped Gloria? You knew about the plan to attack D'Angelo? You knew Charlie was alive?"

Weldon nodded without a word.

Magnolia snapped, "All this time, you lied to me."

"I'm so sorry, Nolia. I know I should have told you, but I wanted your reactions to the events to be real so Cavanaugh wouldn't realize I was spying on him. He had to believe I was helping him destroy you and your friends," Weldon said.

Magnolia swallowed hard. "What happened at the art museum?"

Weldon held his hands palms up on his lap. "I didn't start the fire, Nolia. I locked you in planning to leave and that's it, but Duffy showed up with the arson kit. I went to the bathroom and called the fire department. Then I ran into Leo and Charlie. Believe me. I was thrilled Leo saved you from that fire."

Magnolia lowered her hands to her lap. Her heart was conflicted. She wanted to believe him. However, his deception had run so deep. *I fell in love with him.*

"Nolia?"

Magnolia mumbled, "I don't agree with what you did, Weldon, but it worked. Thank you for your help in stopping Peter and his minions. I hope you'll always have happiness."

"I will as long as I'm with you."

Magnolia stood up with a shake of her head. "I'm sorry, Weldon, but that's not going to happen."

Weldon struggled to sit up straighter. "Why? I told you I'm sorry. I want to be with you. I love you, Nolia."

Magnolia's heart ached at Weldon's desperate plea. She wished she could forgive him so they could continue their relationship. However, she was deeply hurt by his deception. Her trust in him had been shattered. *How do I know he isn't lying right now?*

Magnolia averted her gaze from Weldon. She turned to make her exit. "Goodbye, Weldon."

Magnolia went through the door swiftly closing it behind her. She leaned on the wall. She blinked away the tears threatening to fall. *Don't be silly, Magnolia Ruby. He never loved you. It was all a lie.*

Sitting on the floor in her living room, Gloria Fairbanks awkwardly waited for D'Quan to say something. She had been thrilled when they had declared their love over the phone. However, neither of them had spoken about it since that day. *Maybe he changed his mind.*

D'Quan said, "Gloria, I wanted to tell you something."

Gloria's heart soared in anticipation. "What?"

D'Quan took a deep breath. He released it loudly. "I told La'Keshia I would have to find a new partner. You mean more to me than the State Science Fair."

"I'm glad, but I already knew. La'Keshia talked to me at school. She wanted to apologize for upsetting me. We're friends now. In fact, we're going shopping this weekend," Gloria explained.

D'Quan sat up straighter. He smiled, "So she can be my science partner?"

"No," snorted Gloria.

D'Quan whined, "But you said you were friends now."

"We are, but that doesn't mean my man can hang out with her."

D'Quan shook his head. He leaned toward his girlfriend. "Okay. Whatever you say. I love you, Gloria."

"I love you too."

The young couple kissed timidly exploring the new phase of their relationship.

"Ew! Gross!"

D'Quan jerked back. He glared at D'Angelo sitting in an armchair watching them.

D'Quan snapped, "Shut up, Rex."

"Big D is so immature," said Gloria rolling her eyes.

Guffawing, D'Angelo slapped a hand on his knee.

Gloria smiled unable to control herself. She liked hearing laughter after so much heartache and stress. *I'm glad we're all safe.*

Magnolia Ruby stirred the pot of mashed potatoes. Her heart wrenched at the loss of the man she had loved. She had returned home not telling anyone about her breakup with Weldon. *I don't want their pity.*

"It's hard, ain't it, honey?"

Magnolia turned from the stove at Camella's question. "What's hard?"

Camella placed hot rolls in a basket. "Love."

Magnolia nodded, "Yes. At least, it was when I was dating Edward."

Camella glanced over at her with raised eyebrows. "I'm not talking about Edward."

"I don't know what you mean, Camella."

Camella sat down at the kitchen table. She motioned for Magnolia to join her.

Once she sat down, Camella patted her arm. "Honey, over the last few months, you have been so happy. You are in love with Mr. Weldon. Anyone can see that."

"Even if that was true, it doesn't matter. I talked to Weldon. He doesn't really love me. It's over," mumbled Magnolia.

"I'm sorry, Magnolia. Nothing hurts more than a broken heart."

Nodding, Magnolia said, "True, but even a broken heart will heal." *Someday.*

Chuckling, D'Angelo Walker listened to D'Quan and Gloria lecture him for spying on their sweet moment. He raised his hands in defeat. He turned his gaze from the young couple.

D'Shontae and Davion looked at their phones showing funny videos to each other.

D'Angelo sighed in contentment. He cherished the safety his family had found. Cavanaugh was dead. His minions would be going to prison.

Closing his eyes, D'Angelo leaned his head against the back of the chair. *Life is perfect.*

Smirking, D'Shontae Walker watched D'Angelo sleep. His older brother snored in the armchair on the other side of the living room.

D'Shontae turned his head to Davion to point out the funny scene. He frowned at the tears in the other one's eyes. *What happened? We were laughing a few minutes ago.*

"What's wrong, Treks?"

Davion mumbled, "I found my mom's obituary. I guess her cousin wrote it. I'm not mentioned in the list of survivors."

D'Shontae cringed at the pain in his voice. He put an arm around Davion's shoulders pulling him closer. "I'm sorry, Treks. I know it hurts."

"How do I make it stop hurting, Hex?"

D'Shontae frowned. Was there a way to make it stop? He snapped his eyes to D'Angelo as the sleeping man snored loudly. He glanced over at D'Quan whispering with Gloria. He peered into the open kitchen doorway seeing Big Mama helping Ms. Magnolia cook. *I know how to make the hurting stop.*

"You have to hold onto your new family," D'Shontae said.

Davion nodded, "I think I can do that."

Charlotte Pearl sat on the porch swing outside Mags' house enjoying the sunset. She sighed pleased the group had survived their final game with Peter Cavanaugh.

Charlotte lowered her eyes from the sky at a car door.

Frankie and Leo marched up the walkway bantering with each other.

"Case officially closed?" asked Charlotte.

Frankie snorted, "You bet. Time for a home-cooked meal."

Charlotte motioned toward the house. "Big Mama and Mags have been working on it for over an hour. I don't think you will be disappointed."

"Lemmons would eat an old tire if it had hot sauce," snorted Leo.

Frankie slammed a teasing fist into his arm. She headed for the front door. "And I wouldn't share it with you, Knight."

Charlotte beamed at the two partners.

Frankie entered the house.

Leo turned to join his girlfriend on the porch swing. He sat down beside her.

Charlotte leaned in for a kiss.

Leo said, "What are you doing out here?"

"Waiting for you. Have you heard from your mother?" Charlotte replied.

Leo nodded, "They made it home safely. She said she would be in touch soon to reschedule our dinner."

"She's persistent," Charlotte mumbled.

"You have no idea. What do you think?"

Charlotte said, "Maybe we can wait until things have settled down for us. Peter's gone, but I could use a break from stress."

Leo took her hand into his own. He raised it up to tenderly kiss it. "We can all use a break. We'll worry about my mother later."

Dropping her hand, Leo glanced around. "Besides, I don't know if I want you around my mother so soon after all this. You have quite a power of wielding a meat thermometer."

Slapping his arm, Charlotte snorted, "Wow. Don't quit your day job, Leo. You would never make it as a comedian."

"How rude! You better be nice to me. I'm the only one who can protect you from my mother," Leo said.

Charlotte replied, "Not if I have a meat thermometer."

Chuckling, Leo took her hand into his own intertwining their fingers.

The door opened with a bang. Charlotte jerked at the loud sound. She turned her head then smiled.

Frankie snapped, "Would you two get in here so we can eat? I'm starving."

EPILOGUE

TENSE TALK

Magnolia Ruby sat on the couch beside Charlie. Her heavy heart plagued her. She thanked God for their survival and the end of Peter Cavanaugh's games. They were lucky to be alive. The loss of Weldon hurt her, but she focused on the rest of her family and friends.

The doorbell rang. Magnolia tensed. She was not expecting anyone. The Walkers were here. Frankie and Leo had already arrived. Who was missing?

Motioning for Gloria to let her answer it, Magnolia stood. She strolled to the front door. Opening it, her concern melted away.

"Hello, Lucretia. Please come in," Magnolia said stepping to the side to give her room.

Gloria's aunt entered the house. She scanned the living room. "Thank goodness you are all safe."

Gloria stood from her place on the floor. She rushed over to hug her aunt. "We're fine. It's finally over."

Magnolia sat down on the couch. She echoed Gloria's relief at the Peter Cavanaugh nightmare ending.

Lucretia moved to stand at the middle of the room. She looked at each person for a moment as if assessing the situation.

Magnolia tilted her head at the odd behavior. What was she doing?

Lucretia said, "I want to say something."

Magnolia folded her hands on her lap. Her temper flared at her tone. Lucretia was a guest in her house. Yet, she was taking over the gathering.

At Lucretia's glance, Magnolia nodded. She bit her lip fearing what she would say. Tact was not her strong suit.

Lucretia said, "A I look at all of you, it is obvious to me that you have faced too much ugliness over the last few months if not longer."

Magnolia nodded. What was her point? She waited. She could always jump in if Lucretia took it too far.

Lucretia added, "What you need is a vacation and that is exactly what you are going to have."

Magnolia relaxed. She had planned to spend some time without crime and horrors.

Lucretia said, "I have rented a large cabin at the Heavenly Hideaways lake resort for next week. There's a fall break at school so Gloria and D'Quan can come. The rest of you will need to put in for a week off."

Magnolia tensed at the command. She glanced over at the others. Their faces showed exactly how they felt about Lucretia bossing them around.

Lucretia snapped her gaze back to her. She smiled sweetly, "What do you think, Magnolia?"

"Well…"

Lucretia asked, "Doesn't a week at the lake sound better than staying in the city where crime and murder pop up into your lives too often?"

"It sounds nice," Magnolia admitted.

Clapping her hands once, Lucretia said, "Then it's settled. Everyone, make arrangements. We leave on Saturday."

Magnolia's forehead wrinkled at the last statement. Was Lucretia planning to go to the lake with them? It would be rude to exclude her since she was paying for them all to go. If Lucretia wanted to be a part of the family, then Magnolia could be kind enough to include her.

Magnolia turned her head to ask the others what they wanted to do. She tilted her head. They were all looking at her for her reaction. When had she become the head of the family?

Taking a deep breath, Magnolia said, "I think that sounds perfect. Thank you, Lucretia."

As the others agreed then started to chatter about the fun they could have at a lake, Magnolia smiled warmly. She liked the idea of a week relaxing by a lake. No worries. No reminders of Weldon. No murders. No psychopaths. Only peace and quiet. Time to relax and heal. *It's a vacation. What could go wrong?*

ABOUT THE AUTHOR

Carrie Rachelle Johnson has always enjoyed reading a variety of fictional genres. She loves to curl up in her recliner with a good book. It is no surprise Carrie decided to try her hand at storytelling in multiple genres as well.

Carrie spends much of her time worshiping and serving the Lord at her home church. She is very involved in several children's ministries. Carrie also enjoys teaching at an elementary school in Missouri. She spends her free time with family, friends, and creating new stories for her fans.

Carrie is the author of the other Magnolia Ruby novels as well as The Glory Chronicles series which is a fantasy allegory for our spiritual journey. She has also published Lyric's List and Stranded Treasure which are Christian romance novels.

Carrie would love to hear from her readers. Be sure to check out Carrie Rachelle Johnson on Facebook or email her at carrierachellejohnson@outlook.com!

SNEAK PREVIEW OF

MAGNOLIA RUBY MYSTERY #11

Officer Frankie Lemmons climbed out of her patrol car. She walked next to her partner to the crime scene. They had been called to the house for a possible domestic violence case. A neighbor had reported loud noises and screams from the house. *I hope we're not too late.*

Frankie placed her hand on her holstered Glock. She stood on the porch of the house. Glancing at her partner, she knocked on the door. "Police!"

Silence. Frankie knocked harder. "Police! Open the door or we'll bust it in!"

"Really, Lemmons."

Frankie shrugged, "What? It might convince someone to cooperate."

The door creaked open a few inches. Frankie tilted her head. "I'm Officer Lemmons. This is Officer Kent. We received a report of loud noises. May we come in?"

The door opened wider. A young woman with new bruises on her face and neck stepped to the side. She averted her gaze from the police officers. "Ella Foster."

Frankie entered the house. She scanned the living room with beer bottles scattered around on the floor. A coffee table was stationed on its side. There was a lamp with the shade laying next to the base.

"Mrs. Foster, is your husband home?" Frankie asked.

"No."

Frankie nodded, "Do you want to press charges?"

"For what?"

Frankie stared at her. How could she pretend like nothing had happened?

Kent cleared his throat. "How did you get the bruises, ma'am?"

The woman crossed her arms. She stared at the floor. "I fell down the stairs."

Frankie's eyes widened at the lie. There was no way the woman had received her injuries falling down the stairs. Someone had clearly hit her. "We can't help you if you don't tell us the truth, Mrs. Foster."

The woman raised her head. Glaring at her, she hissed, "Are you calling me a liar?"

Moving to stand in front of Frankie, Kent said, "No, ma'am. Do you need medical treatment?"

"I'm fine. Please just leave. My husband's a lawyer. He won't like how you have treated me."

Frankie opened her mouth with a retort about how Mr. Foster treated his wife. She bit back her response. Her eyes narrowed at Kent as he motioned for her to leave the house.

Kent said, "Have a good evening, ma'am."

As the door slammed behind them, Frankie glowered at her partner. "What was that?"

"That was you messing up the case," Kent mumbled.

"What?"

Kent said, "Look, Lemmons. Your lack of tact caused that woman to shut down. She wasn't going to tell us the truth now for anything."

"I was trying to nail the guy who beat the crap out of her," Frankie snapped.

"By insulting the battered woman? Nice strategy," Kent snorted.

Frankie marched toward the car. She hated being with a partner who never had her back. Why couldn't she be teamed up with a cop willing to do what it took to bust a criminal? "We should at least call in a detective and let them investigate."

"Let it go, Lemmons. No detective is going to force the truth out of that woman," said Kent.

Frankie snorted, "I would."

"Oh, please. You'll never make it to detective. You can't even control yourself on a routine call."

Frankie bit her lip. She wished she could snap back with a retort. However, the truth was he was right. She had messed up by insinuating Mrs. Foster was lying. Her mouth had ruined her chances of helping her. Who knows what would happen to the woman with her husband free to return home and abuse her?

Climbing into the front passenger seat of their patrol car, Frankie mumbled, "Mark my words. He'll kill her one of these days."

Made in the USA
Coppell, TX
05 June 2021

56880016R00069